Lion!

●

We suddenly rounded a point, to see the lion lying in a box-like space in the wall. The shelf ended there. I had once before been confronted with a like situation, and had expected to find it here, so was not frightened. The lion looked up from his task of licking a bloody paw and uttered a fierce growl. His tail began to lash to and fro; it knocked the little stones off the shelf. I heard them click on the wall. Again and again he spat, showing great, white fangs. He was a Tom, heavy and large.

ZANE GREY

ROPING LIONS IN THE GRAND CANYON

TOR®

A TOM DOHERTY ASSOCIATES BOOK
NEW YORK

This is a work of fiction. All the characters and events portrayed in this book are fictitious, and any resemblance to real people or events is purely coincidental.

ROPING LIONS IN THE GRAND CANYON

A Tor Book
Published by Tom Doherty Associates, LLC
175 Fifth Avenue
New York, NY 10010

www.tor.com

Tor® is a registered trademark of Tom Doherty Associates, LLC.

ISBN: 0-812-56353-0

First Tor edition: May 1996

Printed in the United States of America

0 9 8 7 6 5 4 3 2

Introduction

•

To the Boy Scouts of America and Readers of this Book:

In bringing out this volume, *Roping Lions in the Grand Canyon*, I wish to make clear the fact that this is a story of my actual experiences with Buffalo Jones, the last of the plainsmen. My boy readers will doubtless find some of the material familiar, for in my book, *The Young Lion Hunter*, I incorporated many of the incidents in the adventures of Ken Ward.

That was fiction: this is the true story.

I am hoping that it may influence boys to a keener love and appreciation of all the wonderful outdoors of their native land.

Every boy has a heritage. It is outdoor America. Our open country, that is to say, our uncultivated lands,

ROPING LIONS IN THE GRAND CANYON

● ● ●

forests, preserves, feeding and nesting swamps, are threatened by the march of so-called progress and commercialism. What is needed is two million Boy Scouts to save some of our green, fragrant, untrammeled land for the boys to come.

The Scout movement is one of the most splendid developments of young America. Through it the future generations will learn how to fare in the outdoors, and will study the great lessons that nature teaches. To love hikes and camps and horses and dogs, to seek the wild creatures with more desire to study them than to kill, to learn to accomplish with the hands, to meet difficult situations that arise, to endure pain and privation, to cultivate strength of body and simplicity of mind—these are the things that make a good Scout.

So, in putting out this volume of *Roping Lions in the Grand Canyon*, it is with the hope that its readers will find more than merely entertainment between its covers; that the stories of lions and wild horses and deer, the descriptions of wonderful forestland and rugged grandeur of canyons, and particularly the memory of that strange and remarkable man, Buffalo Jones, preserver of the American bison, and a great plainsman, will generate the impulse which may help to preserve our great outdoors for future generations.

—ZANE GREY
Spring, 1924

1

The Grand Canyon of Arizona is over two hundred miles long, thirteen wide, and a mile and a half deep; a titanic gorge in which mountains, tablelands, chasms and cliffs lie half veiled in purple haze. It is wild and sublime, a thing of wonder, of mystery; beyond all else a place to grip the heart of a man, to unleash his daring spirit.

On April 20, 1908, after days on the hot desert, my weary party and pack train reached the summit of Powell's Plateau, the most isolated, inaccessible and remarkable mesa of any size in all the canyon country. Cut off from the mainland, it appeared insurmountable; standing aloof from the towers and escarpments, rugged and bold in outline, its forest

● ● ●

covering like a strip of black velvet, its giant granite walls gold in the sun, it seemed apart from the world, haunting with its beauty, isolation and wild promise.

The members of my party harmoniously fitted the scene. Buffalo Jones, burly-shouldered, bronze-faced, and grim, proved in his appearance what a lifetime on the plains could make of a man. Emett was a Mormon, a massively built gray-bearded son of the desert; he had lived his life on it; he had conquered it and in his falcon eyes shone all its fire and freedom. Ranger Jim Owens had the wiry, supple body and careless, tidy garb of the cowboy, and the watchful gaze, quiet face and locked lips of the frontiersman. The fourth member was a Navajo Indian, a copper-skinned, raven-haired, black-eyed desert warrior.

I had told Emett to hire someone who could put the horses on grass in the evening and then find them the next morning. In Northern Arizona this required more than genius. Emett secured the best trailer of the desert Navajos. Jones hated an Indian; and Jim, who carried an ounce of lead somewhere in his person, associated this painful addition to his weight with an unfriendly Apache, and swore all Indians should be dead. So between the two, Emett and I had trouble in keeping our Navajo from illustrating the plainsman idea of a really good Indian—a dead one.

While we were pitching camp among magnificent pine trees, and above a hollow where a heavy bank of

● ● ●

snow still lay, a sodden pounding in the turf attracted our attention.

"Hold the horses!" yelled Emett.

As we all made a dive among our snorting and plunging horses the sound seemed to be coming right into camp. In a moment I saw a string of wild horses thundering by. A noble black stallion led them, and as he ran with beautiful stride he curved his fine head backward to look at us, and whistled his wild challenge.

Later a herd of large white-tailed deer trooped up the hollow. The Navajo grew much excited and wanted me to shoot, and when Emett told him we had not come out to kill, he looked dumfounded. Even the Indian felt it a strange departure from the usual mode of hunting to travel and climb hundreds of miles over hot desert and rock-ribbed canyons, to camp at last in a spot so wild that deer were tame as cattle, and then not kill.

Nothing could have pleased me better, incident to the settling into permanent camp. The wild horses and tame deer added the all-satisfying touch to the background of forest, flowers and mighty pines and sunlit patches of grass; the white tents and red blankets, the sleeping hounds and blazing fire-logs, all making a picture like that of a hunter's dream.

"Come, saddle up," called the never restful Jones. "Leave the Indian in camp with the hounds, and

● ● ●

we'll get the lay of the land." All afternoon we spent riding the plateau. What a wonderful place! We were completely bewildered with its physical properties, and surprised at the abundance of wild horses and mustangs, deer, coyotes, foxes, grouse and other birds, and overjoyed to find innumerable lion trails. When we returned to camp I drew a rough map, which Jones laid flat on the ground as he called us around him.

"Now, boys, let's get our heads together."

In shape the plateau resembled the ace of clubs. The center and side wings were high and well wooded with heavy pines; the middle wing was longest, sloped west, had no pine, but a dense growth of cedar. Numerous ridges and canyons cut up this central wing. Middle Canyon, the longest and deepest, bisected the plateau, headed near camp, and ran parallel with two smaller ones, which we named Right and Left Canyons. These three were lion runways and hundreds of deer carcasses lined the thickets. North Hollow was the only depression, as well as runway, on the northwest rim. West Point formed the extreme western cape of the plateau. To the left of West Point was a deep cut-in of the rim wall, called the Bay. The three important canyons opened into it. From the Bay, the south rim was regular and impassable all the way round to the narrow Saddle, which connected it to the mainland.

ROPING LIONS IN THE GRAND CANYON

● ● ●

"Now, then," said Jones, when we assured him that we were pretty well informed as to the important features, "you can readily see our advantage. The plateau is about nine or ten miles long, and six wide at its widest. We can't get lost, at least for long. We know where lions can go over the rim and we'll head them off, make shortcut chases, something new in lion hunting. We are positive the lions cannot get over the second wall, except where we came up, at the Saddle. In regard to lion signs, I'm doubtful of the evidence of my own eyes. This is virgin ground. No white man or Indian has ever hunted lions here. We have stumbled on a lion home, the breeding place of hundreds of lions that infest the north rim of the canyon."

The old plainsman struck a big fist into the palm of his hand, a rare action with him. Jim lifted his broad hat and ran his fingers through his white hair. In Emett's clear desert-eagle eyes shone a furtive, anxious look, which yet could not overshadow the smouldering fire.

"If only we don't kill the horses!" he said.

More than anything else that remark from such a man thrilled me with its subtle suggestion. He loved those beautiful horses. What wild rides he saw in his mind's eye! In cold calculation we perceived the wonderful possibilities never before experienced by

5

● ● ●

hunters, and as the wild spell clutched us my last bar of restraint let down.

During supper we talked incessantly, and afterward around the campfire. Twilight fell with the dark shadows sweeping under the silent pines; the night wind rose and began its moan.

"Shore there's some scent on the wind," said Jim, lighting his pipe with a red ember. "See how oneasy Don is."

The hound raised his fine, dark head and repeatedly sniffed the air, then walked to and fro as if on guard for his pack. Moze ground his teeth on a bone and growled at one of the pups. Sounder was sleepy, but he watched Don with suspicious eyes. The other hounds, mature and somber, lay stretched before the fire.

"Tie them up, Jim," said Jones, "and let's turn in."

2

When I awakened next morning the sound of Emett's axe rang out sharply. Little streaks of light from the campfire played between the flaps of the tent. I saw old Moze get up and stretch himself. A jangle of cowbells from the forest told me we would not have to wait for the horses that morning.

"The Injun's all right," Jones remarked to Emett.

"All rustle for breakfast," called Jim.

We ate in the semidarkness with the gray shadow ever brightening. Dawn broke as we saddled our horses. The pups were limber, and ran to and fro on their chains, scenting the air; the older hounds stood quietly waiting.

"Come, Navvy—come chase cougie," said Emett.

● ● ●

"Dam'! No!" replied the Indian.

"Let him keep camp," suggested Jim.

"All right; but he'll eat us out," Emett declared.

"Climb up, you fellows," said Jones, impatiently. "Have I got everything—rope, chains, collars, wire, nippers? Yes, all right. Hyar, you lazy dogs—out of this!"

We rode abreast down the ridge. The demeanor of the hounds contrasted sharply with what it had been at the start of the hunt the year before. Then they had been eager, uncertain, violent; they did not know what was in the air; now they filed after Don in an orderly trot.

We struck out of the pines at half past five. Floating mist hid the lower end of the plateau. The morning had a cool touch but there was no frost. Crossing Middle Canyon about halfway down, we jogged on. Cedar trees began to show bright green against the soft gray sage. We were nearing the dark line of the cedar forest when Jim, who led, held up his hand in a warning check. We closed in around him.

"Watch Don," he said.

The hound stood stiff, head well up, nose working, and the hair on his back bristling. All the other hounds whined and kept close to him.

"Don scents a lion," whispered Jim. "I've never known him to do that unless there was the scent of a lion on the wind."

ROPING LIONS IN THE GRAND CANYON

● ● ●

"Hunt 'em up, Don, old boy," called Jones.

The pack commenced to work back and forth along the ridge. We neared a hollow when Don barked eagerly. Sounder answered and likewise Jude. Moze's short angry "bow-wow" showed the old gladiator to be in line.

"Ranger's gone," cried Jim. "He was farthest ahead. I'll bet he's struck it. We'll know in a minute, for we're close."

The hounds were tearing through the sage, working harder and harder, calling and answering one another, all the time getting down into the hollow.

Don suddenly let out a string of yelps. I saw him running head up, pass into the cedars like a yellow dart. Sounder howled his deep, full bay, and led the rest of the pack up the slope in angry clamor.

"They're off!" yelled Jim, and so were we.

In less than a minute we had lost one another. Crashings among the dry cedars, thud of hoofs and yells kept me going in one direction. The fiery burst of the hounds had surprised me. I remembered that Jim had said Emett and his charger might keep the pack in sight, but that none of the rest of us could.

It did not take me long to realize what my mustang was made of. His name was Foxie, which suited him well. He carried me at a fast pace on the trail of someone; and he seemed to know that by keeping in this trail part of the work of breaking through the

9

● ● ●

brush was already done for him. Nevertheless, the sharp dead branches, more numerous in a cedar forest than elsewhere, struck and stung us as we passed. We climbed a ridge, and found the cedars thinning out into open patches. Then we faced a bare slope of sage and I saw Emett below on his big horse.

Foxie bolted down this slope, hurdling the bunches of sage, and showing the speed of which Emett had boasted. The open ground, with its brush, rock and gullies, was easy going for the little mustang. I heard nothing save the wind singing in my ears. Emett's trail, plain in the yellow ground, showed me the way. On entering the cedars again I pulled Foxie in and stopped twice to yell "Waa-hoo!" I heard the baying of the hounds, but no answer to my signal. Then I attended to the stern business of catching up. For what seemed a long time I threaded the maze of cedar, galloped the open sage flats, always on Emett's track.

A signal cry, sharp to the right, turned me. I answered, and with the exchange of signal cries found my way into an open glade where Jones and Jim awaited me.

"Here's one," said Jim. "Emett must be with the hounds. Listen."

With the labored breathing of the horses filling our ears we could hear no other sound. Dismounting, I went aside and turned my ear to the breeze.

"I hear Don," I cried instantly.

● ● ●

"Which way?" both men asked.

"West."

"Strange," said Jones. "The hound wouldn't split, would he, Jim?"

"Don leave that hot trail? Shore he wouldn't," replied Jim. "But his runnin' do seem queer this morning."

"The breeze is freshening," I said. "There! Now listen! Don, and Sounder, too."

The baying came closer and closer. Our horses threw up long ears. It was hard to sit still and wait. At a quick cry from Jim we saw Don cross the lower end of the flat.

No need to spur our mounts! The lifting of bridles served, and away we raced. Foxie passed the others in short order. Don had long disappeared, but with blended bays, Jude, Moze, and Sounder broke out of the cedars hot on the trail. They, too, were out of sight in a moment.

The crash of breaking brush and thunder of hoofs from where the hounds had come out of the forest attracted and even frightened me. I saw the green of a low cedar tree shake, and split, to let out a huge, gaunt horse with a big man doubled over his saddle. The onslaught of Emett and his desert charger stirred a fear in me that checked admiration.

"Hounds running wild," he yelled, and the dark shadows of the cedars claimed him again.

ROPING LIONS IN THE GRAND CANYON
● ● ●

A hundred yards within the forest we came again upon Emett, dismounted, searching the ground. Moze and Sounder were with him, apparently at fault. Suddenly Moze left the little glade and, venting his sullen quick bark, disappeared under the trees. Sounder sat on his haunches and yelped.

"Now what the hell is wrong?" growled Jones, tumbling off his saddle.

"Shore something is," said Jim, also dismounting.

"Here's a lion track," interposed Emett.

"Ha! and here's another," cried Jones, in great satisfaction. "That's the trail we were on, and here's another crossing it at right angles. Both are fresh; one isn't fifteen minutes old. Don and Jude have split one way and Moze another. By George! that's great of Sounder to hang fire!"

"Put him on the fresh trail," said Jim, vaulting into his saddle.

Jones complied, with the result that we saw Sounder start off on the trail Moze had taken. All of us got in some pretty hard riding, and managed to stay within earshot of Sounder. We crossed a canyon, and presently reached another which, from its depth, must have been Middle Canyon. Sounder did not climb the opposite slope, so we followed the rim. From a bare ridge we distinguished the line of pines above us, and decided that our location was in about the center of the plateau.

ROPING LIONS IN THE GRAND CANYON

● ● ●

Very little time elapsed before we heard Moze. Sounder had caught up with him. We came to a halt where the canyon widened and was not so deep, with cliffs and cedars opposite us, and an easy slope leading down. Sounder bayed incessantly; Moze emitted harsh, eager howls, and both hounds, in plain sight, began working in circles.

"The lion has gone up somewhere," cried Jim. "Look sharp!"

Repeatedly Moze worked to the edge of a low wall of stone and looked over; then he barked and ran back to the slope, only to return. When I saw him slide down a steep place, make for the bottom of the stone wall, and jump into the low branches of a cedar, I knew where to look. Then I descried the lion, a round yellow ball, cunningly curled up in a mass of dark branches. He had leaped into the tree from the wall.

"There he is! Treed! Treed!" I yelled. "Moze has found him."

"Down, boys, down into the canyon," shouted Jones, in sharp voice. "Make a racket; we don't want him to jump."

How he and Jim and Emett rolled and cracked the stone! For a moment I could not get off my horse; I was chained to my saddle by a strange vacillation that could have been no other thing than fear.

"Are you afraid?" called Jones from below.

13

● ● ●

"Yes, but I am coming," I replied, and dismounted to plunge down the hill. It may have been shame or anger that dominated me then; whatever it was I made directly for the cedar, and did not halt until I was under the snarling lion.

"Not too close!" warned Jones. "He might jump. It's a Tom, a two-year-old, and full of fight."

It did not matter to me then whether he jumped or not. I knew I had to be cured of my dread, and the sooner it was done the better.

Old Moze had already climbed a third of the distance up to the lion.

"Hyar, Moze! Out of there, you rascal coon chaser!" Jones yelled as he threw stones and sticks at the hound. Moze, however, replied with his snarly bark and climbed on steadily.

"I've got to pull him out. Watch close, boys, and tell me if the lion starts down."

When Jones climbed the first few branches of the tree, Tom let out an ominous growl.

"Make ready to jump. Shore he's comin'," called Jim.

The lion, snarling viciously, started to descend. It was a ticklish moment for all of us, particularly Jones. Warily he backed down.

"Boys, maybe he's bluffing," said Jones. "Try him out. Grab sticks and run at the tree and yell, as if you were going to kill him."

ROPING LIONS IN THE GRAND CANYON

● ● ●

Not improbably the demonstration we executed under the tree would have frightened even an African lion. Tom hesitated, showed his white fangs, returned to his first perch, and from there climbed as far as he could. The forked branch on which he stood swayed alarmingly.

"Here, punch Moze out," said Jim, handing up a long pole.

The old hound hung like a leech to the tree, making it difficult to dislodge him. At length he fell heavily, and, venting his thick battle cry, attempted to climb again.

Jim seized him, made him fast to the rope with which Sounder had already been tied.

"Say, Emett, I've no chance here," called Jones. "You try to throw at him from the rock."

Emett ran up the rock, coiled his lasso and cast the noose. It sailed perfectly in between the branches and circled Tom's head. Before it could be slipped tight he had thrown it off. Then he hid behind the branches.

"I'm going farther up," said Jones.

"Be quick," yelled Jim.

Jones evidently had that in mind. When he reached the middle fork of the cedar, he stood erect and extended the noose of his lasso on the point of his pole. Tom, with a hiss and snap, struck at it savagely. The second trial tempted the lion to saw the rope with his

15

● ● ●

teeth. In a flash Jones withdrew the pole, and lifted a loop of the slack rope over the lion's ears.

"Pull!" he yelled.

Emett, at the other end of the lasso, threw his great strength into action, pulling the lion out with a crash, and giving the cedar such a tremendous shaking that Jones lost his footing and fell heavily.

Thrilling as the moment was, I had to laugh, for Jones came up out of a cloud of dust, as angry as a wet hornet, and made prodigious leaps to get out of the reach of the whirling lion.

"Look out—!" he bawled.

Tom, certainly none the worse for his tumble, made three leaps, two at Jones, one at Jim, which were checked by the short length of the rope in Emett's hands. Then for a moment a thick cloud of dust enveloped the wrestling lion, during which the quick-witted Jones tied the free end of the lasso to a sapling.

"Dod gast the luck!" yelled Jones, reaching for another lasso. "I didn't mean for you to pull him out of the tree. Now he'll get loose or kill himself."

When the dust cleared away, we discovered our prize stretched out at full length and frothing at the mouth. As Jones approached, the lion began a series of evolutions so rapid as to be almost indiscernible to the eye. I saw a wheel of dust and yellow fur. Then came a thud and the lion lay inert.

• • •

Jones pounced upon him and loosed the lasso around his neck.

"I think he's done for, but maybe not. He's breathing yet. Here, help me tie his paws together. Look out! He's coming to!"

The lion stirred and raised his head. Jones ran the loop of the second lasso around the two hind paws and stretched the lion out. While in this helpless position and with no strength and hardly any breath left in him the lion was easy to handle. With Emett's help Jones quickly clipped the sharp claws, tied the four paws together, took off the neck lasso and substituted a collar and chain.

"There, that's one. He'll come to, all right," said Jones. "But we are lucky. Emett, never pull another lion clear out of a tree. Pull him over a limb and hang him there while someone below ropes his hind paws. That's the only way, and if we don't stick to it, somebody is going to get done for. Come, now, we'll leave this fellow here and hunt up Don and Jude. They've treed another lion by this time."

Remarkable to me was to see how, as soon as the lion lay helpless, Sounder lost his interest. Moze growled, yet readily left the spot. Before we reached the level, both hounds had disappeared.

"Hear that?" yelled Jones, digging spurs into his horse. "Hi! Hi! Hi!"

From the cedars rang the thrilling, blending chorus

17

● ● ●

of bays that told of a treed lion. The forest was almost impenetrable. We had to pick our way. Emett forged ahead; we heard him smashing the deadwood; and soon a yell proclaimed the truth of Jones's assertion.

First I saw the men looking upward; then Moze climbing the cedar, and the other hounds with noses skyward; and last, in the dead top of the tree, a dark blot against the blue, a big tawny lion.

"Whoop!" The yell leaped past my lips. Quiet Jim was yelling; and Emett, silent man of the desert, let from his wide cavernous chest a booming roar that drowned ours.

Jones's next decisive action turned us from exultation to the grim business of the thing. He pulled Moze out of the cedar, and while he climbed up, Emett ran his rope under the collars of all of the hounds. Quick as the idea flashed over me I leaped into the cedar adjoining the one Jones was in, and went up hand over hand. A few pulls brought me to the top, and then my blood ran hot and quick, for I was level with the lion, too close for comfort, but in excellent position for taking pictures.

The lion, not heeding me, peered down at Jones, between widespread paws. I could hear nothing except the hounds. Jones's gray hat came pushing up between the dead snags; then his burly shoulders. The quivering muscles of the lion gathered tense, and

● ● ●

his lithe body crouched low on the branches. He was about to jump. His open dripping jaws, his wild eyes, roving in terror for some means of escape, his tufted tail, swinging against the twigs and breaking them, manifested his extremity. The eager hounds waited below, howling, leaping.

It bothered me considerably to keep my balance, regulate my camera and watch the proceedings. Jones climbed on with his rope between his teeth, and a long stick. The very next instant, it seemed to me, I heard the cracking of branches and saw the lion biting hard at the noose which circled his neck.

Here I swung down, branch to branch, and dropped to the ground, for I wanted to see what went on below. Above the howls and yelps, I distinguished Jones's yell. Emett ran directly under the lion with a spread noose in his hands. Jones pulled and pulled, but the lion held on firmly. Throwing the end of the lasso down to Jim, Jones yelled again, and then they both pulled. The lion was too strong. Suddenly, however, the branch broke, letting the lion fall, kicking frantically with all four paws. Emett grasped one of the four whipping paws, and even as the powerful animal sent him staggering he dexterously left the noose fast on the paw. Jim and Jones in unison let go of their lasso, which streaked up through the branches as the lion fell, and then it dropped to the ground, where Jim made a flying grab for it. Jones, plunging out of the tree, fell upon the rope at the same instant.

If the action up to then had been fast, it was slow to what followed. It seemed impossible for two strong men with one lasso, and a giant with another, to straighten out that lion. He was all over the little space under the trees at once. The dust flew, the sticks snapped, the gravel pattered like shot against the cedars. Jones plowed the ground flat on his stomach, holding on with one hand, with the other trying to fasten the rope to something; Jim went to his knees; and on the other side of the lion, Emett's huge bulk tipped a sharp angle, and then fell.

I shouted and ran forward, having no idea what to do, but Emett rolled backward at the same instant the other men got a strong haul on the lion. Short as that moment was in which the lasso slackened, it sufficed for Jones to make the rope fast to a tree. Whereupon with the three men pulling on the other side of the leaping lion, somehow I had flashed into my mind the game that children play, called skipping the rope, for the lion and lasso shot up and down.

This lasted for only a few seconds. They stretched the beast from tree to tree, and Jones, running with the third lasso, made fast the front paws.

"It's a female," said Jones, as the lion lay helpless, her sides swelling; "a good-sized female. She's

● ● ●

nearly eight feet from tip to tip, but not very heavy. Hand me another rope."

When all four lassos had been stretched, the lioness could not move. Jones strapped a collar around her neck and clipped the sharp yellow claws.

"Now to muzzle her," he continued.

Jones's method of performing this most hazardous part of the work was characteristic of him. He thrust a stick between her open jaws, and when she crushed it to splinters he tried another, and yet another, until he found one that she could not break. Then while she bit on it, he placed a wire loop over her nose, slowly tightening it, leaving the stick back of her big canines.

The hounds ceased their yelping and, when untied, Sounder wagged his tail as if to say, "Well done," and then lay down; Don walked within three feet of the lion, as if she were now beneath his dignity; Jude began to nurse and lick her sore paw; only Moze the incorrigible retained antipathy for the captive, and he growled, as always, low and deep. And on the moment, Ranger, dusty and lame from travel, trotted wearily into the glade and, looking at the lioness, gave one disgusted bark and flopped down.

3

Transporting our captives to camp bade fair to make us work. When Jones, who had gone after the pack horses, hove in sight on the sage flat, it was plain to us that we were in for trouble. The bay stallion was on the rampage.

"Why didn't you fetch the Indian?" growled Emett, who lost his temper when matters concerning his horses went wrong. "Spread out, boys, and head him off."

We contrived to surround the stallion, and Emett succeeded in getting a halter on him.

"I didn't want the bay," explained Jones, "but I couldn't drive the others without him. When I told

● ● ●

that redskin that we had two lions, he ran off into the woods, so I had to come alone."

"I'm going to scalp the Navajo," said Jim, complacently.

These remarks were exchanged on the open ridge at the entrance to the thick cedar forest. The two lions lay just within its shady precincts. Emett and I, using a long pole in lieu of a horse, had carried Tom up from the canyon to where we had captured the lioness.

Jones had brought a packsaddle and two panniers. When Emett essayed to lead the horse which carried these, the animal stood straight up and began to show some of his primal desert instincts. It certainly was good luck that we unbuckled the packsaddle straps before he left the vicinity. In about three jumps he had separated himself from the panniers, which were then placed upon the back of another horse. This one, a fine-looking beast, and amiable under surroundings where his life and health were considered even a little, immediately disclaimed any intention of entering the forest.

"They scent the lions," said Jones. "I was afraid of it; never had but one nag that would pack lions."

"Maybe we can't pack them at all," replied Emett dubiously. "It's certainly new to me."

"We've got to," Jones asserted; "try the sorrel."

For the first time in a serviceable and honorable

● ● ●

life, according to Emett, the sorrel broke his halter and kicked like a plantation mule.

"It's a matter of fright. Try the stallion. He doesn't look afraid," said Jones, who never knew when he was beaten.

Emett gazed at Jones as if he had not heard right.

"Go ahead, try the stallion. I like the way he looks."

No wonder! The big stallion looked a king of horses—just what he would have been if Emett had not taken him, when a colt, from his wild desert brothers. He scented the lions, and he held his proud head up, his ears erect, and his large, dark eyes shone fiery and expressive.

"I'll try to lead him in and let him see the lions. We can't fool him," said Emett.

Marc showed no hesitation, nor anything we expected. He stood stiff-legged, and looked as if he wanted to fight.

"He's all right; he'll pack them," declared Jones.

The packsaddle being strapped on and the panniers hooked to the horns, Jones and Jim lifted Tom and shoved him down into the left pannier while Emett held the horse. A madder lion than Tom never lived. It was cruel enough to be lassoed and disgrace enough to be "hog-tied," as Jim called it, but to be thrust down into a bag and packed on a horse was adding insult to injury. Tom frothed at the mouth and

24

● ● ●

seemed like a fizzing torpedo about to explode. The lioness, being considerably longer and larger, was with difficulty gotten into the other pannier, and her head and paws hung out. Both lions kept growling and snarling.

"I look to see Marc bolt over the rim," said Emett, resignedly, as Jones took up the end of the rope halter.

"No, siree!" sang out that worthy. "He's helping us out; he's proud to show up the other nags."

Jones was always asserting strange traits in animals, and giving them intelligence and reason. As to that, many incidents coming under my observation while with him, and seen with his eyes, made me incline to his claims, the fruit of a lifetime with animals.

Marc packed the lions to camp in short order, and, quoting Jones, "without turning a hair." We saw the Navajo's head protruding from a tree. Emett yelled for him, and Jones and Jim "ha-haed" derisively; whereupon the black head vanished and did not reappear. Then they unhooked one of the panniers and dumped out the lioness. Jones fastened her chain to a small pine tree, and as she lay powerless he pulled out the stick back of her canines. This allowed the wire muzzle to fall off. She signaled this freedom with a roar that showed her health to be still unimpaired. The last action in releasing her from her pain-

● ● ●

ful bonds Jones performed with sleight-of-hand dexterity. He slipped the loop fastening one paw, which loosened the rope, and in a twinkling let her work all of her other paws free. Up she sprang, ears flat, eyes ablaze, mouth wide, once more capable of defense, true to her instinct and her name.

Before the men lowered Tom from Marc's back I stepped closer and put my face within six inches of the lion's. He promptly spat on me. I had to steel my nerve to keep so close. But I wanted to see a wild lion's eyes at close range. They were exquisitely beautiful, their physical properties as wonderful as their expression. Great half globes of tawny amber, streaked with delicate wavy lines of black, surrounding pupils of intense purple fire. Pictures shone and faded in the amber light—the shaggy tipped plateau, the dark pines and smoky canyons, the great dotted downward slopes, the yellow cliffs and crags. Deep in those live pupils, changing, quickening with a thousand vibrations, quivered the soul of this savage beast, the wildest of all wild Nature, unquenchable love of life and freedom, flame of defiance and hate.

Jones disposed of Tom in the same manner as he had the lioness, chaining him to an adjoining small pine, where he leaped and wrestled.

Presently I saw Emett coming through the woods leading and dragging the Indian. I felt sorry for the Navvy, for I felt that his fear was not so much physi-

● ● ●

cal as spiritual. And it seemed no wonder to me that the Navvy should hang back from this sacrilegious treatment of his god. A natural wisdom, which I had in common with all human beings who consider self-preservation the first law of life, deterred me from acquainting my august companions with my belief. At least I did not want to break up the camp.

In the remorseless grasp of Emett, forced along, the Navajo dragged his feet and held his face side-wise, though his dark eyes gleamed at the lions. Terror predominated among the expressions of his countenance. Emett drew him within fifteen feet and held him there, and with voice, and gesticulating of his free hand, tried to show the poor fellow that the lions would not hurt him.

Navvy stared and muttered to himself. Here Jim had some deviltry in mind, for he edged up closer; but what it was never transpired, for Emett suddenly pointed to the horses and said to the Indian:

"*Chineago* (feed)."

It appeared when Navvy swung himself over Marc's broad back, that our great stallion had laid aside his transiently noble disposition and was himself again. Marc proceeded to show us how truly Jim had spoken: "Shore he ain't no use for the Indian." Before the Indian had fairly gotten astride, Marc dropped his head, humped his shoulders, brought his feet together and began to buck. Now the Navajo was

● ● ●

a famous breaker of wild mustangs, but Marc was a tougher proposition than the wildest mustang that ever romped the desert. Not only was he unusually vigorous; he was robust and heavy, yet exceedingly active. I had seen him roll over in the dust three times each way, and do it easily—a feat Emett declared he had never seen performed by another horse.

Navvy began to bounce. He showed his teeth and twisted his sinewy hands in the horse's mane. Marc began to act like a demon; he plowed the ground; apparently he bucked five feet straight up. As the Indian had bounced he now began to shoot into the air. He rose the last time with his heels over his head, to the full extent of his arms; and on plunging down his hold broke. He spun around the horse, then went hurtling to the ground some twenty feet away. He sat up, and seeing Emett and Jones laughing, and Jim prostrated with joy, he showed his white teeth in a smile and said:

"No bueno dam'."

I think all of us respected Navvy for his good humor, and especially when he walked up to Marc and, with no show of the mean Indian, patted the glossy neck and then nimbly remounted. Marc, not being so difficult to please as Jim in the way of discomfiting the Navajo, appeared satisfied for the present, and trotted off down the hollow, with the string of horses ahead, their bells jingling.

ROPING LIONS IN THE GRAND CANYON

• • •

Camp-fire tasks were a necessary wage in order to earn the full enjoyment and benefit of the hunting trip; and looking for some task to which to turn my hand, I helped Jim feed the hounds. To feed ordinary dogs is a matter of throwing them a bone; however, our dogs were not ordinary. It took time to feed them, and a prodigious amount of meat. We had packed between three and four hundred pounds of wild-horse meat, which had been cut into small pieces and strung on the branches of a scrub oak near camp.

Don, as befitted a gentleman and the leader of the greatest pack in the West, had to be fed by hand. I believe he would rather have starved than have demeaned himself by fighting. Starved he certainly would have, if Jim had thrown meat indiscriminately to the ground. Sounder asserted his rights and preferred large portions at a time. Jude begged with great solemn eyes, but was no slouch at eating, for all her gentleness. Ranger, because of imperfectly developed teeth rendering mastication difficult, had to have his share cut into very small pieces. As for Moze—well, great dogs have their faults as do great men—he never got enough meat; he would fight even poor crippled Jude, and steal even from the pups; when he had gotten all Jim would give him, and all he could snatch, he would growl away with bulging sides.

"How about feeding the lions?" asked Emett.

● ● ●

"They'll drink tonight," replied Jones, "but won't eat for days; then we'll tempt them with fresh rabbits."

We made a hearty meal, succeeding which Jones and I walked through the woods toward the rim. A yellow promontory, huge and glistening, invited us westward, and after a detour of half a mile we reached it. The points of the rim, striking out into the immense void, always drew me irresistibly. We found the view from this rock one of startling splendor. The corrugated rim wall of the middle wing extended to the west, at this moment apparently running into the setting sun. The gold glare touching up the millions of facets of chiseled stone, created color and brilliance too glorious and intense for the gaze of men. And looking downward was like looking into the placid, blue, bottomless depths of the Pacific.

"Here, help me push off this stone," I said to Jones. We heaved a huge round stone, and were encouraged to feel it move. Fortunately we had a little slope; the boulder groaned, rocked and began to slide. Just as it toppled over I glanced at the second hand of my watch. Then with eyes over the rim we waited. The silence was the silence of the canyon, dead and vast, intensified by our breathless earstrain. Ten long palpitating seconds and no sound! I gave up. The distance was too great for sound to reach us. Fifteen seconds—seventeen—eighteen—

● ● ●

With that a puff of air seemed to rise, and on it the most awful bellow of thunderous roar. It rolled up and widened, deadened to burst out and roll louder, then slowly, like mountains on wheels, rumbled under the rim walls, passing on and on, to roar back in echo from the cliffs of the mesas. Roar and rumble—roar and rumble! for two long moments the dull and hollow echoes rolled at us, to die away slowly in the far-distant canyons.

"That's a darned deep hole," commented Jones.

Twilight stole down on us idling there, silent, content to watch the red glow pass away from the buttes and peaks, the color deepening downward to meet the ebon shades of night creeping up like a dark tide.

On turning toward the camp we essayed a shortcut, which brought us to a deep hollow with stony walls, which seemed better to go around. The hollow, however, was quite long and we decided presently to cross it. We descended a little way when Jones suddenly barred my progress with his big arm.

"Listen," he whispered.

It was quiet in the woods; only a faint breeze stirred the pine needles; and the weird, gray darkness seemed to be approaching under the trees.

I heard the patter of light, hard hoofs on the scaly sides of the hollow.

"Deer?" I asked my companion in a low voice.

"Yes; see," he replied, pointing ahead, "just right

● ● ●

under that broken wall of rock; right there on this side; they're going down."

I descried gray objects the color of the rocks, moving down like shadows.

"Have they scented us?"

"Hardly; the breeze is against us. Maybe they heard us break a twig. They've stopped, but they are not looking our way. Now I wonder—"

Rattling of stones set into movement by some quick, sharp action, an indistinct crash, but sudden, as of the impact of soft, heavy bodies, a strange wild sound preceded in rapid succession violent brushings and thumpings in the scrub of the hollow.

"Lion jumped a deer," yelled Jones. "Right under our eyes! Come on! Hi! Hi! Hi!"

He ran down the incline yelling all of the way, and I kept close to him, adding my yells to his, and gripping my revolver. Toward the bottom the thicket barred our progress so that we had to smash through and I came out a little ahead of Jones. And farther up the hollow I saw a gray swiftly bounding object too long and too low for a deer, and I hurriedly shot six times at it.

"By George! Come here," called my companion. "How's this for quick work? It's a yearling doe."

In another moment I leaned over a gray mass huddled at Jones's feet. It was a deer, gasping and choking. I plainly heard the wheeze of blood in its throat,

● ● ●

and the sound, like a death-rattle, affected me powerfully. Bending closer, I saw where one side of the
neck, low down, had been terribly lacerated.

"Waa-hoo!" pealed down the slope.

"That's Emett," cried Jones, answering the signal.
"If you have another shot put this doe out of agony."

But I had not a shot left, nor did either of us have
a clasp knife. We stood there while the doe gasped
and quivered. The peculiar sound, probably made by
the intake of air through the laceration of the throat,
on the spur of the moment seemed pitifully human.

I felt that the struggle for life and death in any living thing was a horrible spectacle. With great interest
I had studied natural selection, the variability of animals under different conditions of struggling exis-
tence, the law whereby one animal struck down and
devoured another. But I had never seen and heard
that law enacted on such a scale; and suddenly I ab-
horred it.

Emett strode to us through the gathering darkness.

"What's up?" he asked quickly.

He carried my Remington in one hand and his
Winchester in the other; and he moved so assuredly
and loomed up so big in the dusk that I experienced
a sudden little rush of feeling as to what his advent
might mean at a time of real peril.

"Emett, I've lived to see many things," replied

ROPING LIONS IN THE GRAND CANYON

• • •

Jones, "but this is the first time I ever saw a lion jump a deer right under my nose!"

As Emett bent over to seize the long ears of the deer, I noticed the gasping had ceased.

"Neck broken," he said, lifting the head. "Well, I'm danged. Must have been an all-fired strong lion. He'll come back, you may be sure of that. Let's skin out the quarters and hang the carcass up in a tree!"

We returned to camp in half an hour, the richer for our walk by a quantity of fresh venison. Upon being acquainted with our adventure, Jim expressed himself rather more fairly than was his customary way.

"Shore that beats hell! I knowed there was a lion somewheres, because Don wouldn't lie down. I'd like to get a pop at the brute."

I believed Jim's wish found an echo in all our hearts. At any rate to hear Emett and Jones express regret over the death of the doe justified in some degree my own feelings, and I thought it was not so much the death, but the lingering and terrible manner of it, and especially how vividly it connoted the wild-life drama of the plateau. The tragedy we had all but interrupted occurred every night, perhaps often in the day and likely at different points at the same time. Emett told how he had found fourteen piles of bleached bones and dried hair in the thickets of less than a mile of the hollow on which we were encamped.

ROPING LIONS IN THE GRAND CANYON

• • •

"We'll rope the danged cats, boys, or we'll kill them."

"It's blowing cold. Hey, Navvy, *coco! coco!*" called Emett.

The Indian, carefully laying aside his cigarette, kicked up the fire and threw on more wood.

"*Dicass!* (cold)," he said to me. "*Coco, bueno* (fire good)."

I replied, "Me savvy—yes."

"Sleep-ie?" he asked.

"Mucha," I returned.

While we carried on a sort of novel conversation full of Navajo, English, and gestures, darkness settled down black. I saw the stars disappear; the wind changing to the north, grew colder and carried a breath of snow. I like north wind best—from under the warm blankets—because of the roar and lull and lull and roar in the pines. Crawling into the bed presently, I lay there and listened to the rising storm-wind for a long time. Sometimes it swelled and crashed like the sound of a breaker on the beach, but mostly, from a low incessant moan, it rose and filled to a mighty rush, then suddenly lulled. This lull, despite a wakeful, thronging mind, was conducive to sleep.

4

To be awakened from pleasant dreams is the lot of man. The Navajo aroused me with his singing, and when I peeped languidly from under the flap of my sleeping bag, I felt a cold air and saw fleecy flakes of white drifting through the small window of my tent.

"Snow; by all that's lucky!" I exclaimed, remembering Jones's hopes. Straightway my languor vanished and getting into my boots and coat I went outside. Navvy's bed lay in six inches of snow. The forest was beautifully white. A fine dazzling snow was falling. I walked to the roaring campfire. Jim's biscuits, well browned and of generous size, had just been dumped into the middle of our breakfast cloth, a tarpaulin spread on the ground; the coffee pot

● ● ●

steamed fragrantly, and a Dutch oven sizzled with a great number of slices of venison.

"Did you hear the Indian chanting?" asked Jones, who sat with his horny hands to the blaze.

"I heard his singing."

"No, it wasn't a song; the Navajo never sings in the morning. What you heard was his morning prayer, a chant, a religious and solemn ritual to the break of day. Emett says it is a custom of the desert tribe. You remember how we saw the Mokis sitting on the roofs of their little adobe huts in the gray of the morning. They always greet the sun in that way. The Navajos chant."

It certainly was worth remembering, I thought, and mentally observed that I would wake up thereafter and listen to the Indian.

"Good luck and bad!" went on Jones. "Snow is what we want, but now we can't find the scent of our lion of last night."

Low growls and snarls attracted me. Both our captives presented sorry spectacles; they were wet, dirty, bedraggled. Emett had chopped down a small pine, the branches of which he was using to makc shelter for the lions. While I looked on Tom tore his to pieces several times, but the lioness crawled under hers and began licking her chops. At length Tom, seeing that Emett meant no underhand trick, backed out of the drizzling snow and lay down.

ROPING LIONS IN THE GRAND CANYON

● ● ●

Emett had already constructed a shack for the hounds. It was a way of his to think of everything. He had the most extraordinary ability. A stroke of his axe, a twist of his great hands, a turn of this or that made camp a more comfortable place. And if something, no matter what, got out of order or broken, there was Emett to show what it was to be a man of the desert. It had been my good fortune to see many able men on the trail and round the campfire, but not one of them even approached Emett's class. When I said a word to him about his knack with things, his reply was illuminating: "I'm fifty-eight, and four out of every five nights of my life I have slept away from home on the ground."

"Chineago!" called Jim, who had begun with all of us to assimilate a little of the Navajo's language.

Whereupon we fell to eating with appetite unknown to any save hunters. Somehow the Indian had gravitated to me at mealtimes, and now he sat cross-legged beside me, holding out his plate and looking as hungry as Moze. At first he had always asked for the same kind of food that I happened to have on my own plate. When I had finished and had no desire to eat more, he gave up his faculty of imitation and asked for anything he could get. The Navajo had a marvelous appetite. He liked sweet things, sugar best of all. It was a fatal error to let him get his hands on a can of fruit. Although he inspired Jones with disgust and Jim with worse, he was a source of unfailing pleasure to me. He called me "Mista Gay" and he pronounced the words haltingly in low voice and with unmistakable respect.

"What's on for today?" queried Emett.

"I guess we may as well hang around camp and rest the hounds," replied Jones. "I did intend to go after the lion that killed the deer, but this snow has taken away the scent."

"Shore it'll stop snowin' soon," said Jim.

The falling snow had thinned out and looked like flying powder; the leaden clouds, rolling close to the treetops, grew brighter and brighter; bits of azure sky shone through rifts.

Navvy had tramped off to find the horses, and not long after his departure he sent out a prolonged yell that echoed through the forest.

"Something's up," said Emett instantly. "An Indian never yells like that at a horse."

We waited quietly for a moment, expecting to hear the yell repeated. It was not, though we soon heard the jangle of bells, which told us he had the horses coming. He appeared off to the right, riding Foxie and racing the others toward camp.

"Cougie—mucha big—dam'!" he said, leaping off the mustang to confront us.

"Emett, does he mean he saw a cougar or a track?" questioned Jones.

● ● ●

"Me savvy," replied the Indian. *"Butteen, butteen!"*

"He says, trail—trail," put in Emett. "I guess I'd better go and see."

"I'll go with you," said Jones. "Jim, keep the hounds tight and hurry with the horses' oats."

We followed the tracks of the horses, which led southwest toward the rim, and a quarter of a mile from camp we crossed a lion trail running at right angles with our direction.

"Old Sultan!" I cried, breathlessly, recognizing that the tracks had been made by a giant lion we had named Sultan. They were huge, round, and deep, and with my spread hand I could not reach across one of them.

Without a word, Jones strode off on the trail. It headed east and after a short distance turned toward camp. I suppose Jones knew what the lion had been about, but to Emett and me it was mystifying. Two hundred yards from camp we came to a fallen pine, the body of which was easily six feet high. On the side of this log, almost on top, were two enormous lion tracks, imprinted in the mantle of snow. From here the trail led off northeast.

"Darn me!" ejaculated Jones. "The big critter came right into camp; he scented our lions, and raised up on this log to look over."

Wheeling, he started for camp on the trot. Emett

● ● ●

and I kept even with him. Words were superfluous. We knew what was coming. A made-to-order lion trail could not have equaled the one right in the back yard of our camp.

"Saddle up!" said Jones, with the sharp inflection of words that had come to thrill me. "Jim, old Sultan has taken a look at us since break of day."

I got into my chaps, rammed my little automatic into its saddle holster and mounted. Foxie seemed to want to go. The hounds came out of their sheds and yawned, looking at us knowingly. Emett spoke a word to the Navajo, and then we were trotting down through the forest. The sun had broken out warm, causing water to drip off the snow-laden pines. The three of us rode close behind Jones, who spoke low and sternly to the hounds.

What an opportunity to watch Don! I wondered how soon he would catch the scent of the trail. He led the pack as usual and kept to a leisurely dogtrot. When within twenty yards of the fallen log, he stopped for an instant and held up his head, though without exhibiting any suspicion or uneasiness.

The wind blew strong at our backs, a circumstance that probably kept Don so long in ignorance of the trail. A few yards further on, however, he stopped and raised his fine head. He lowered it and trotted on, only to stop again. His easy air of satisfaction with the morning suddenly vanished. His savage hunting

● ● ●

instinct awakened through some channel to raise the short yellow hair on his neck and shoulders and make it stand stiff. He stood undecided with warily shifting nose, then jumped forward with a yelp. Another jump brought another sharp cry from him. Sounder, close behind, echoed the yelp. Jude began to whine. Then Don, with a wild howl, leaped ten feet to alight on the lion trail and to break into wonderfully rapid flight. The seven other hounds, bunched in a black and yellow group, tore after him, filling the forest with their wild uproar.

Emett's horse bounded as I have seen a great racer leave the post, and his desert brothers, loving wild bursts of speed, needing no spur, kept their noses even with his flanks. The soft snow, not too deep, rather facilitated than impeded this wild movement, and the open forest was like a highway.

So we rode, bending low in the saddle, keen eyes alert for branches, vaulting the white-blanketed logs, and swerving as we split to pass the pines. The mist from the melting snow moistened our faces, and the rushing air cooled them with fresh, soft sensation. There were moments when we rode abreast and others when we sailed single file, with white ground receding, vanishing behind us.

My feeling was one of glorious excitation in the swift, smooth flight and a grim assurance of soon seeing the old lion. But I hoped we would not rout

● ● ●

him too soon from under a windfall, or a thicket where he had dragged a deer, because the race was too splendid a thing to cut short. Through my mind whirled with inconceivable rapidity the great lion chases on which we had ridden the year before. And this was another chase, only more stirring, more beautiful, because it was the nature of the thing to grow always with experience.

Don slipped out of sight among the pines. The others strung along the trail, glinted across the sunlit patches. The black pup was neck and neck with Ranger. Sounder ran at their heels, leading the other pups. Moze dashed on doggedly ahead of Jude.

But for us to keep to the open forest, close to the hounds, was not in the nature of a lion chase. Old Sultan's trail turned due west when he began to go down the little hollows and their intervening ridges. We lost ground. The pack left us behind. The slope of the plateau became decided. We rode out of the pines to find the snow failing in the open. Water ran in little gullies and glistened on the sagebrush. A half mile further down the snow had gone. We came upon the hounds running at fault, except Sounder, and he had given up.

"All over," sang out Jones, turning his horse. "The lion's track and his scent have gone with the snow. I reckon we'll do as well to wait until tomorrow. He's

43

● ● ●

down in the middle wing somewhere and it is my idea we might catch his trail as he comes back."

The sudden dashing aside of our hopes was exasperating. There seemed no help for it; abrupt endings to exciting chases were but features of the lion hunt. The warm sun had been hours on the lower end of the plateau, where the snow never lay long; and even if we found a fresh morning trail in the sand, the heat would have burned out the scent.

So rapidly did the snow thaw that by the time we reached camp only the shady patches were left.

It was almost eleven o'clock when I lay down on my bed to rest awhile and fell asleep. The tramp of a horse awakened me. I heard Jim calling Jones. Thinking it was time to eat, I went out. The snow had all disappeared and the forest was brown as ever. Jim sat on his horse and Navvy appeared riding up to the hollow, leading the saddle horses.

"Jones, get out," called Jim.

"Can't you let a fellow sleep? I'm not hungry," replied Jones testily.

"Get out and saddle up," continued Jim.

Jones burst out of his tent, with rumpled hair and sleepy eyes.

"I went over to see the carcass of the deer an' found a lion sittin' up in the tree, feedin' for all he was worth. He jumped out an' ran up the hollow an'

over the rim. So I rustled back for you fellows.
Lively now, we'll get this one sure."

"Was it the big fellow?" I asked.

"No, but he ain't no kitten; an' he's a fine color, sort
of reddish. I never seen one just as bright. Where's
Emett?"

"I don't know. He was here a little while ago.
Shall I signal for him?"

"Don't yell," cried Jones, holding up his fingers. "Be
quiet now."

Without another word we finished saddling,
mounted and, close together, with the hounds in
front, rode through the forest toward the rim.

5

We rode in different directions toward the hollow, the better to chance meeting with Emett, but none of us caught a glimpse of him.

It happened that when we headed into the hollow it was at a point just above where the deer carcass hung in the scrub oak. Don, in spite of Jones's stern yells, let out his eager hunting yelp and darted down the slope. The pack bolted after him and in less than ten seconds were racing up the hollow, their thrilling, blending bays a welcome spur to action. Though I spoke not a word to my mustang nor had time to raise the bridle, he wheeled to one side and began to run. The other horses also kept to the ridge, as I could tell by the pounding of hoofs on the soft turf.

ROPING LIONS IN THE GRAND CANYON

● ● ●

The hounds in full cry right under us urged our good steeds to a terrific pace. It was well that the ridge afforded clear going.

The speed at which we traveled, however, fast as it was, availed not to keep up with the pack. In a short half mile, just as the hollow sloped and merged into level ground, they left us behind and disappeared so quickly as almost to frighten me. My mustang plunged out of the forest to the rim and dashed along, apparently unmindful of the chasm. The red and yellow surface blurred in a blinding glare. I heard the chorus of hounds, but as its direction baffled me I trusted to my horse and I did well, for soon he came to a dead halt on the rim.

Then I heard the hounds below me. I had but time to see the character of the place—long, yellow promontories running out and slopes of weathered stone reaching up between to a level with the rim—when in a dwarf pine growing just over the edge I caught sight of a long, red, pantherish body.

I whooped to my followers now close upon me and, leaping off, hauled out my Remington and ran to the cliff. The lion's long, slender body, of a rare golden-red color, bright, clean, black-tipped and white-bellied, proclaimed it a female of exceeding beauty. I could have touched her with a fishing rod and saw how easily she could be roped from where I stood. The tree in which she had taken refuge grew

47

● ● ●

from the head of a weathered slope and rose close to the wall. At that point it was merely a parapet of crumbling yellow rock. No doubt she had lain concealed under the shelving wall and had not had time to get away before the hounds were right upon her.

"She's going to jump," yelled Jones, in my rear, as he dismounted.

I saw a golden-red streak flash downward, heard a mad medley from the hounds, a cloud of dust rose, then something bright shone for a second to the right along the wall. I ran with all my might to a headland of rock upon which I scrambled and saw with joy that I could command the situation.

The lioness was not in sight, nor were the hounds. The latter, however, were hot on the trail. I knew the lioness had taken to another tree or a hole under the wall, and would soon be routed out. This time I felt sure she would run down and I took a rapid glance below. The slope inclined at a steep angle and was one long slide of bits of yellow stone with many bunches of scrub oak and manzanita. Those latter I saw with satisfaction, because in case I had to go down they would stop the little avalanches. The slope reached down perhaps five hundred yards and ended in a thicket and jumble of rocks from which rose on the right a bare yellow slide. This ran up to a low cliff. I hoped the lion would not go that way, for it

● ● ●

led to great broken battlements of rim. Left of the slide was a patch of cedars.

Jim's yell pealed out, followed by the familiar penetrating howl of the pack when it sighted game. With that I saw the lioness leaping down the slope and close behind her a yellow hound.

"Go it, Don, old boy!" I yelled, wild with delight.

A crushing step on the stones told me Jones had arrived.

"Hi! Hi! Hi!" roared he.

I thought then that if the lioness did not cover thirty feet at every jump I was not in a condition to judge distance. She ran away from Don as if he had been tied and reached the thicket below a hundred yards ahead of him. And when Don, leaving his brave pack far up the slide, entered the thicket the lioness came out on the other side and bounded up the bare slope of yellow shale.

"Shoot ahead of her! Head her off! Turn her back!" cried Jones.

With the word I threw forward the Remington and let drive. Following the bellow of the rifle, so loud in that thin air, a sharp, harsh report cracked up from below. A puff of yellow dust rose in front of the lioness. I was in line, but too far ahead. I fired again. The steel-jacketed bullet hit a stone and spitefully whined away into the canyon. I tried once more. This time I struck close to the lioness. Disconcerted by a cloud

● ● ●

of dust rising before her very eyes she wheeled and ran back.

We had forgotten Don and suddenly he darted out of the thicket, straight up the slide. Always, in every chase, we were afraid the great hound would run to meet his death. We knew it was coming sometime. When the lioness saw him and stopped, both Jones and I felt that this was to be the end of Don.

"Shoot her! Shoot her!" cried Jones. "She'll kill him! She'll kill him!"

As I knelt on the rock I had a hard contraction of my throat, and then all my muscles set tight and rigid. I pulled the trigger of my automatic once, twice. It was wonderful how closely the two bullets followed each other, as we could tell by the almost simultaneous puffs of dust rising from under the beast's nose. She must have been showered and stung with gravel, for she bounded off to the left and disappeared in the cedars. I had missed, but the shots had served to a better end than if I had killed her.

As Don raced up the ground where a moment before a battle and probably death had awaited him, the other hounds burst from the thicket. With that, a golden form seemed to stand out from the green of the cedar, to move and to rise.

"She's treed! She's treed!" shouted Jones. "Go down and keep her there while I follow."

From the back of the promontory where I met the

main wall, I let myself down a niche, foot here and there, a hand hard on the soft stone, braced knee and back until I jumped to the edge of the slope. The scrub oak and manzanita saved me many a fall. I set some stones rolling and I beat them to the bottom. Having passed the thicket, I bent my efforts to the yellow slide and when I had surmounted it my breath came in labored pants. The howling of the hounds guided me through the cedars.

First I saw Moze in the branches of cedar and above him the lioness. I ran out into a little open patch of stony ground at the end of which the tree stood leaning over a precipice. In truth the lioness was swaying over a chasm.

Those details I grasped in a glance, then suddenly awoke to the fact that the lioness was savagely snarling at Moze.

"Moze! Moze! Get down!" I yelled.

He climbed on serenely. He was a most exasperating dog. I screamed at him and hit him with a rock big enough to break his bones. He kept on climbing. Here was a predicament. Moze would surely get to the lioness if I did not stop him, and this seemed impossible. It was out of the question for me to climb after him. And if the lioness jumped she would have to pass me or come straight at me. So I slipped down the safety catch on my automatic and stood ready to save Moze or myself.

ROPING LIONS IN THE GRAND CANYON
● ● ●

The lioness, with a show of fury that startled me, descended her branch a few steps, and reaching below gave Moze a sounding smack with her big paw. The hound dropped as if he had been shot and hit the ground with a thud. Whereupon she returned to her perch.

This reassured me and I ran among the dogs and caught Moze already starting for the tree again and tied him, with a strap I always carried, to a small bush nearby. I heard the yells of my companions and looking back over the tops of the cedars I saw Jim riding down and higher to the left Jones sliding, falling, running at a great rate. I encouraged them to keep up the good work, and then gave my attention to the lioness.

She regarded me with a cold, savage stare and showed her teeth. I repaid this incivility on her part by promptly photographing her from different points.

Jones and Jim were on the spot before I expected them and both were dusty and dripping with sweat. I found to my surprise that my face was wet, as was also my shirt. Jones carried two lassos, and my canteen, which I had left on the promontory.

"Ain't she a beauty?" he panted, wiping his face. "Wait—till I get my breath."

When finally he walked toward the cedar the lioness stood up and growled as if she realized the entrance of the chief actor upon the scene. Jones cast

● ● ●

his lasso apparently to try her out, and the noose spread out and fell over her head. As he tightened the rope the lioness backed down behind a branch.

"Tie the dogs!" yelled Jones.

"Quick!" added Jim. "She's goin' to jump."

Jim had only time to aid me in running my lasso under the collar of Don, Sounder, Jude, and one of the pups. I made them fast to a cedar. I got my hands on Ranger just as Moze broke his strap. I grabbed his collar and held on.

Right there was where trouble commenced for me. Ranger tussled valiantly and Moze pulled me all over the place. Behind me I heard Jones's roar and Jim's yell; the breaking of branches, the howling of the other dogs. Ranger broke away from me and so enabled me to get my other hand on the neck of crazy Moze. On more than one occasion I had tried to hold him and had failed; this time I swore I would do it if he rolled me over the precipice. As to that, only a bush saved me.

More and louder roars and yells, hoarser howls and sharper wrestling, snapping sounds told me what was going on while I tried to subdue Moze. I had a grim thought that I would just as lief have had hold of the lioness. The hound presently stopped his plunging, which gave me an opportunity to look about. The little space was smoky with a smoke of dust. I saw the lioness stretched out with one lasso around a bush and another around a cedar with the end in the hands of Jim. He looked as if he had dug up the ground. While he tied this lasso securely Jones proceeded to rope the dangerous front paws.

The hounds quieted down and I took advantage of this absence of tumult to get rid of Moze.

"Pretty lively," said Jones, spitting gravel as I walked up. Sand and dust lay thick in his beard and blackened his face. "I tell you she made us root."

Either the lioness had been much weakened or choked, or Jones had unusual luck, for we muzzled her and tied up her paws in short order.

"Where's Ranger?" I asked suddenly, missing him from the panting hounds.

"I grabbed him by the heels when he tackled the lion, and I gave him a sling somewheres," replied Jim.

Ranger put in an appearance then, under the cedars, limping painfully.

"Jim, darn me if I don't believe you pitched him over the precipice!" said Jones.

Examination proved this surmise to be correct. We saw where Ranger had slipped over a twenty-foot wall. If he had gone over just under the cedar where the depth was much greater he would never have come back.

"The hounds are choking with dust and heat," I said. When I poured just a little water from my can-

● ● ●

teen into the crown of my hat, the hounds began
fighting around and over me and spilled the water.

"Behave, you coyotes!" I yelled. Either they were
insulted or fully realized the exigency of the situation, for each one came up and gratefully lapped
every drop of his portion.

"Shore now comes the hell of it," said Jim, appearing with a long pole. "Packin' the critter out."

An argument arose in regard to the best way up the
slope, and by virtue of a majority we decided to try
the direction Jim and I thought best. My companions
led the way, carrying the lioness suspended on the
pole. I brought up the rear, packing my rifle, camera,
lasso, canteen and a chain.

It was killing work. We had to rest every few
steps. Often we would fall. Jim laughed, Jones swore,
and I groaned. Sometimes I had to drop my things to
help my companions. So we toiled wearily up the
loose, steep way.

"What's she shakin' like that for?" asked Jim suddenly.

Jones let down his end of the pole and turned
quickly. Little tremors quivered over the lissome
body of the lioness.

"She's dying," cried Jim, jerking out the stick between her teeth and slipping off the wire muzzle.

Her mouth opened and her frothy tongue lolled
out. Jones pointed to her quivering sides and then

● ● ●

raised her eyelids. We saw the eyes already glazing, solemnly fixed.

"She's gone," he said.

Very soon she lay inert and lifeless. Then we sat beside her without a word, and we could hardly for the moment have been more stunned and heartbroken if it had been the tragic death of one of our kind. In that wild environment, obsessed by the desire to capture those beautiful cats alive, the fateful ending of the successful chase was felt out of all proportion.

"Shore she's dead," said Jim. "And wasn't she a beauty? What was wrong?"

"The heat and lack of water," replied Jones. "She choked. What idiots we were! Why didn't we think to give her a drink?"

So we passionately protested against our want of forethought, and looked again and again with the hope that she might come to. But death had stilled the wild heart. We gave up presently, still did not move on. We were exhausted, and all the while the hounds lay panting on the rocks, the bees hummed, the flies buzzed. The red colors of the upper walls and the purple shades of the lower darkened silently.

6

"Shore we can't set here all night," said Jim. "Let's skin the lion an' feed the hounds."

The most astonishing thing in our eventful day was the amount of meat stowed away by the dogs. Lion flesh appealed to their appetites. If hungry Moze had an ounce of meat, he had ten pounds. It seemed a good opportunity to see how much the old gladiator could eat; and Jim and I cut chunks of meat as fast as possible. Moze gulped them with absolute unconcern of such a thing as mastication. At length he reached his limit, possibly for the first time in his life, and looking longingly at a juicy red strip Jim held out, he refused it with manifest shame. Then he wobbled and fell down.

We called to him as we started to climb the slope,

● ● ●

but he did not come. Then the business of conquering that ascent of sliding stone absorbed all our faculties and strength. Little headway could we have made had it not been for the brush. We toiled up a few feet only to slide back, and so it went on until we were weary of life.

When one by one we at last gained the rim and sat there to recover breath, the sun was a half globe of fire burning over the western ramparts. A red sunset bathed the canyon in crimson, painting the walls, tinting the shadows to resemble dropping mists of blood. It was beautiful and enthralling to my eyes, but I turned away because it wore the mantle of tragedy.

Dispirited and worn out, we trooped into camp to find Emett and a steaming supper. Between bites the three of us related the story of the red lioness. Emett whistled long and low and then expressed his regret in no light terms.

"Roping wild steers and mustangs is play to this work," he said in conclusion.

I was too tired to tease our captive lions that evening; even the glowing campfire tempted me in vain, and I crawled into my bed with eyes already glued shut.

A heavy weight on my feet stirred me from oblivion. At first, when only half awake, I could not realize what had fallen on my bed, then hearing a deep groan I knew Moze had come back. I was dropping off again when a strange, low sound caused my eyes to open

• • •

wide. The black night had faded to the gray of dawn. The sound I recognized at once to be the Navajo's morning chant. I lay there and listened. Soft and monotonous, wild and swelling, but always low and strange, the savage song to the break of day was exquisitely beautiful and harmonious. I wondered what the literal meaning of his words could have been. The significance needed no translation. To the black shadows fading away, to the brightening of the gray light, to the glow of the east, to the morning sun, to the Giver of Life—to these the Indian chanted his prayer.

Could there have been a better prayer? Pagan or not, the Navajo with his forefathers felt the spiritual power of the trees, the rocks, the light and sun, and he prayed to that which was divinely helpful to him in all the mystery of his unintelligible life.

We did not crawl out that morning as early as usual, for it was to be a day of rest. When we did, a mooted question arose—whether we or the hounds were the more crippled. Ranger did not show himself; Don could just walk, and that was all; Moze was either too full or too tired to move; Sounder nursed a foot and Jude favored her lame leg.

After lunch we brightened up somewhat and set ourselves different tasks. Jones had misplaced or lost his wire and began to turn the camp topsy-turvy in his impatient efforts to locate it. The wire, however, was not to be found. This was a calamity, for, as we

● ● ●

asked each other, how could we muzzle lions without wire? Moreover, a half dozen heavy leather straps which I had bought in Kanab for use as lion collars had disappeared. We had only one collar left, the one that Jones had put on the red lioness.

Whereupon we began to blame each other, to argue, to grow heated, and naturally from that to become angry. It seems a fatality of campers along a wild trail, like explorers in an unknown land, to be prone to fight. If there is an explanation of this singular fact, it must be that men at such time lose their poise and veneer of civilization; in brief, they go back. At all events we had it hot and heavy, with the center of attack gradually focusing on Jones, and as he was always losing something, naturally we united in force against him.

Fortunately, we were interrupted by yells from the Navajo off in the woods. The brushing of branches and pounding of hoofs preceded his appearance. In some remarkable manner he had gotten a bridle on Marc, and from the way the big stallion hurled his huge bulk over logs and through thickets, it appeared evident he meant to usurp Jim's ambition and kill the Navajo. Hearing Emett yell, the Indian turned Marc toward camp. The horse slowed down when he neared the glade and tried to buck. But Navvy kept his head up. With that Marc seemed to give way to ungovernable rage and plunged right through camp;

● ● ●

he knocked over the dogs' shelter and thundered down the ridge.

Now the Navajo with the bridle in his hand was thoroughly at home. He was getting his revenge on Marc, and he would have kept his seat on a wild mustang, but Marc swerved suddenly under a low branch of a pine, sweeping the Indian off.

When Navvy did not rise we began to fear he had been seriously hurt, perhaps killed, and we ran to where he lay.

Face downward, hands outstretched, with no movement of body or muscle, he certainly appeared dead.

"Badly hurt," said Emett, "probably back broken. I have seen it before from just such accidents."

"Oh no!" cried Jones, and I felt so deeply I could not speak. Jim, who always wanted Navvy to be a dead Indian, looked profoundly sorry.

"He's a dead Indian, all right," replied Emett.

We rose from our stooping postures and stood around, uncertain and deeply grieved, until a mournful groan from Navvy afforded us much relief.

"That's your dead Indian," exclaimed Jones.

Emett stooped again and felt the Indian's back and got in reward another mournful groan.

"It's his back," said Emett, and true to his ruling passion forever to minister to the needs of horses, men, and things, he began to rub the Indian and call for the liniment.

● ● ●

Jim went to fetch it, while I, still believing the Navvy to be dangerously hurt, knelt by him and pulled up his shirt, exposing the hollow of his brown back.

"Here we are," said Jim, returning on the run with the bottle.

"Pour some on," replied Emett.

Jim removed the cork and soused the liniment all over the Indian's back.

"Don't waste it," remonstrated Emett, starting to rub Navvy's back.

Then occurred a most extraordinary thing. A convulsion seemed to quiver through the Indian's body; he rose at a single leap, and uttering a wild, piercing yell broke into a run. I never saw an Indian or anybody else run so fleetly. Yell after yell pealed back to us.

Absolutely dumfounded, we all gazed at each other.

"That's your dead Indian!" ejaculated Jim.

"What the hell!" exclaimed Emett, who seldom used such language.

"Look here!" cried Jones, grabbing the bottle. "See! Don't you see it?"

Jim fell face downward and began to shake.

"What?" shouted Emett and I together.

"Turpentine, you idiots! Turpentine! Jim brought the wrong bottle!"

In another second three more forms lay stretched out on the sward, and the forest rang with sounds of mirth.

7

That night the wind switched and blew cold from the north, and so strong that the campfire roared like a furnace. "More snow," was the verdict of all of us, and in view of this, I invited the Navajo to share my tent.

"Sleepie-me," I said to him.

"Me savvy," he replied, and forthwith proceeded to make his bed with me.

Much to my surprise, all my comrades raised protestations, which struck me as being singularly selfish, considering they would not be inconvenienced in any way.

"Why not?" I asked. "It's a cold night. There'll be frost, if not snow."

● ● ●

"Shore you'll get 'em," said Jim.

"There never was an Indian that didn't have 'em," added Jones.

"What?" I questioned.

They made mysterious signs that rather augmented my ignorance as to what I might get from the Indian, but in no wise changed my mind. When I went to bed I had to crawl over Navvy. Moze lay at my feet as usual, and he growled so deep that I could not but think he, too, resented the addition to my small tent.

"Mista Gay!" came in the Indian's low voice.

"Well, Navvy?" I asked.

"Sleepie—sleepie?"

"Yes, Navvy, sleepy and tired. Are you?"

"Me savvy—mucha sleepie—mucha—no bueno."

I did not wonder at his feeling sleepy, tired and bad. He did not awaken me in the morning, for when my eyes unclosed the tent was light and he had gone. I found my companions up and doing.

We had breakfast and got into our saddles by the time the sun, a red ball low down among the pines, began to brighten and turn to gold. No snow had fallen, but a thick frost encrusted the ground. The hounds, wearing cloth moccasins, which plainly they detested, trotted in front. Don showed no effects of his great run down the sliding slope after the red lioness; it was one of his remarkable qualities that he recuperated so quickly. Ranger was a little stiff, and

● ● ●

Sounder favored his injured foot. The others were as usual.

Jones led down the big hollow to which he kept after we had passed the edge of the pines; then marking a herd of deer ahead, he turned his horse up the bank.

We breasted the ridge and jogged toward the cedar forest, which we entered without having seen the hounds show interest in anything. Under the cedars in the soft yellow dust we crossed lion tracks, many of them, but too old to carry a scent. Even North Hollow with its regular beaten runway failed to win a murmur from the pack.

"Spread out," said Jones, "and look for tracks. I'll keep the center and hold in the hounds."

Signaling occasionally to one another, we crossed almost the breadth of the cedar forest to its western end, where the open sage flats inclined to the rim. In one of those flats I came upon a broken sagebush, the grass being thick thereabout. I discovered no track, but dismounted and scrutinized the surroundings carefully. A heavy body had been dragged across the sage, crushing it. The ends of broken bushes were green, the leaves showed bruises.

I began to feel like Don when he scented game. Leading my mustang, I slowly proceeded across the open, guided by an occasional down-trodden bush or tuft of grass. As I neared the cedars again Foxie snorted. Under the first tree I found a ghastly bunch

● ● ●

of red bones, a spread of grayish hairs and a split skull. The bones were yet wet; two long doe ears were still warm. Then I saw big lion tracks in the dust and even a well-pressed imprint of a lion's body where he had rolled or lain.

The two yells I sent ringing into the forest were productive of interesting results. Answers came from near and far. Then, what with my calling and the replies, the forest rang so steadily with shrill cries that the echoes had no chance to follow.

An elephant in the jungle could not have caused more crashing and breaking of brush than did Emett as he made his way to me. He arrived from the forest just as Jim galloped across the flat. Mutely I held up the two long ears.

"Get on your horse!" cried Jim after one quick glance at the spread of bones and hair.

It was well he said that, for I might have been left behind. I ran to Foxie and vaulted upon him. A flash of yellow appeared among the sage and a string of yelps split the air.

"It's Don!" yelled Jim.

Well we knew that. What a sight to see him running straight for us! He passed, a savage yellow wolf in his ferocity, and disappeared like a gleam under the gloomy cedars.

We spurred after him. The other hounds sped by. Jones closed in on us from the left, and in a few min-

● ● ●

utes we were strung out behind Emett, fighting the branches, dodging and swerving, hugging the saddle, and always sending out our sharp yells.

The race was furious but short. The three of us coming up together found Emett dismounted on the extreme end of West Point.

"The hounds have gone down," he said, pointing to the runway.

We all listened to the meaning bays.

"Shore they've got him up!" asserted Jim. "Like as not they found him under the rim here, sleeping off his gorge. Now, fellows, I'll go down. It might be a good idea for you to spread along the rim."

With that we turned our horses eastward and rode as close to the rim as possible. Clumps of cedars and deep fissures often forced us to circle them. The hounds, traveling under the walls below, kept pace with us and then forged ahead, which fact caused Jones to dispatch Emett on the gallop for the next runway at North Hollow.

Soon Jones bade me dismount and make my way out upon one of the promontories, while he rode a little farther on. As I tied my mustang I heard the hounds, faint and far beneath. I waded through the sage and cedar to the rim.

Cape after cape jutted out over the abyss. Some were very sharp and bare, others covered with cedar; some tottering crags with a crumbling bridge leading

• • •

to their rims; and some ran down like giant steps. From one of these I watched below. The slope here under the wall was like the side of a rugged mountain. Somewhere down among the dark patches of cedar and the great blocks of stone the hounds were hunting the lion, but I could not see one of them.

The promontory I had chosen had a split, and choked as this was with brush, rock, and shale, it seemed a place where I might climb down. Once started, I could not turn back, and sliding, clinging to what afforded, I worked down the crack. A wall of stone hid the sky from me part of the way. I came out a hundred feet below upon a second promontory of huge slabs of yellow stone. Over these I clambered, to sit with my feet swinging over the last one.

Straight before my gaze yawned the awful expanse of the canyon. In the soft morning light the red mesas, the yellow walls, the black domes were less harsh than in the full noonday sun, purer than in the tender shadow of twilight. Below me were slopes and slides divided by ravines full of stones as large as houses, with here and there a lonesome leaning crag, giving irresistible proof of the downward trend, of the rolling, weathering ruins of the rim. Above, the wall bulged out full of fissures, ragged and rotten shelves, toppling columns of yellow limestone, beaded with quartz and colored by wild flowers wonderfully growing in crannies.

ROPING LIONS IN THE GRAND CANYON

● ● ●

Wild and rare as was this environment, I gave it but a glance and a thought. The bay of the hounds caused me to bend sharp and eager eyes to the open spaces of stone and slide below. Luck was mine as usual; the hounds were working up toward me. How I strained my sight! Hearing a single cry, I looked eastward to see Jones silhouetted against the blue on a black promontory. He seemed a giant primeval man overlooking the ruin of a former world. I signaled him to make for my point.

Black Ranger hove in sight at the top of a yellow slide. He was at fault, but hunting hard. Jude and Sounder bayed off to his left. I heard Don's clear voice, permeating the thin, cool air, seemingly to leave a quality of wildness upon it; yet I could not locate him. Ranger disappeared. Then for a time I only heard Jim. Moze was next to appear, and he, too, was upward bound. A jumble of stone hid him, and then Ranger again showed. Evidently he wanted to get around the bottom of a low crag, for he jumped and jumped, only to fall back.

Quite naturally my eyes searched that crag. Stretched out upon the top of it was the long, slender body of a lion.

"Hi! Hi! Hi! Hi! Hi!" I yelled till my lungs failed me.

"Where are you?" came from above.

"Here! Here!" I cried, seeing Jones on the rim.

69

● ● ●

"Come down. Climb down the crack. The lion is here; on top of that round crag. He's fooled the hounds and they can't find him."

"I see him! I see him!" yelled Jones. Then he roared out a single call for Emett that pealed like a clear clarion along the curved broken rim wall, opening up echoes which clapped like thunder.

While Jones clattered down I turned again to the lion. He lay with head hidden under a little shelf and he moved not a muscle. What a place for him to choose! But for my accidental venturing down the broken fragments and steps of the rim he could have remained safe from pursuit.

Suddenly, right under my feet, Don opened his string of yelps. I could not see him, but decided he must be above the lion on the crag. I leaned over as far as I dared. At that moment among the varied and thrilling sounds about me I became vaguely aware of hard, panting breaths, like coughs, somewhere in my vicinity. As Jones had set in motion bushels of stone and had already scraped his feet over the rocks behind me, I thought the forced respiration came from him. When I turned he was yet far off—too far for me to hear him breathe. I thought this circumstance strange, but straightway forgot it.

On the moment from my right somewhere Don pealed out his bugle blast, and immediately after,

● ● ●

Sounder and Jude joining him, sent up the thrice welcome news of a treed lion.

"There 're two! There 're two!" I yelled to Jones, now working down to my right.

"He's treed down here. I've got him spotted!" replied Jones. "You stay there and watch your lion. Yell for Emett."

Signal after signal for Emett earned no response, though Jim far below to the left sent me an answer.

The next few minutes, or more likely half an hour, passed with Jones and me separated from each other by a wall of broken stone, waiting impatiently for Jim and Emett, while the hounds bayed one lion and I watched the other.

Calmness was impossible under such circumstances. No man could have gazed into that marvel of color and distance, with wild life about him, with wild sounds ringing in his ears, without yielding to the throb and race of his wild blood.

Emett did not come. Jim had not answered a yell for minutes. No doubt he needed his breath. He came into sight just to the left of our position, and he ran down one side of the ravine to toil up the other. I hailed him, Jones hailed him and the hounds hailed him.

"Steer to your left, Jim!" I called. "There's a lion

on that crag above you. He might jump. Round the cliff to the left—Jones is there!"

The most painful task it was for me to sit there and listen to the sound rising from below without being able to see what happened. My lion had peeped up once, and, seeing me, had crouched closer to his crag, evidently believing he was unseen, which obviously made it imperative for me to keep my seat and hold him there as long as possible.

But to hear the various exclamations thrilled me enough.

"Hyar, Moze—get out of that. Catch him—hold him! Damn these rotten limbs. Hand me a pole— Jones, back down—back down! he's comin'—Hi! Hi! Whoop! Boo—o! There—now you've got him! No, no; it slipped! Now! Look out, Jim, from under—he's going to jump!"

A smashing and rattling of loose stones and a fiery burst of yelps with trumpetlike yells followed close upon Jones's last words. Then two yellow streaks leaped down the ravine. The first was the lion, the second was Don. The rest of the pack came tumbling helter-skelter in their wake. Following them raced Jim in long kangaroo leaps, with Jones in the rear, running for all he was worth. The animated and musical procession passed up out of the ravine and gradually lengthened as the lion gained and Jones lost, till it passed altogether from my jealous sight.

ROPING LIONS IN THE GRAND CANYON

● ● ●

On the other side of the ridge of cedars the hounds treed their quarry again, as was easy to tell by their change from sharp intermittent yelping to an unbroken, full, deep chorus. Then presently all quieted down, and for long moments at a time the still silence enfolded the slope. Shouts now and then floated up on the wind, and an occasional bark.

I sat there for an hour by my watch, though it seemed only a few minutes, and all that time my lion lay crouched on his crag and never moved.

I looked across the curve of the canyon to the purple breaks of the Siwash and the shaggy side of Buckskin Mountain and far beyond to where Kanab Canyon opened its dark mouth, and farther still to the Pink Cliffs of Utah, weird and dim in the distance.

Something swelled within my breast at the thought that for the time I was part of that wild scene. The eye of an eagle soaring above would have placed me as well as my lion among the few living things in the range of his all-compassing vision. Therefore, all was mine, not merely the lion—for he was only the means to an end—but the stupendous, unnameable thing beneath me, this chasm that hid mountains in the shades of its cliffs, and the granite tombs, some gleaming pale, passionless, others red and warm, painted by a master hand; and the windcaves, dark-portaled under their mist curtains, and all that was deep and far off, unapproachable, unattainable, of

● ● ●

beauty exceeding, dressed in ever-changing hues, was mine by right of presence, by right of the eye to see and the mind to keep.

"Waa-hoo!"

The cry lifted itself out of the depths. I saw Jones on the ridge of cedars.

"All right here—have you kept your lion there?" he yelled.

"All's well—come along, come along," I replied.

I watched them coming, and all the while my lion never moved. The hounds reached the base of the cliff under me, but they could not find the lion, though they scented him, for they kept up a continual baying. Jim got up to the shelf under me and said they had tied up the lion and left him below. Jones toiled slowly up the slope.

"Someone ought to stay down there; he might jump," I called in warning.

"That crag is forty feet high on this side," he replied.

I clambered back over the uneven mass, let myself down between the boulders and crawled under a dark ridge, and finally, with Jim catching my rifle and camera and then lending his shoulders, I reached the bench below. Jones came puffing around a corner of the cliff, and soon all three of us with the hounds stood out on the rocky shelf with only a narrow space between us and the crouching lion.

ROPING LIONS IN THE GRAND CANYON

● ● ●

Before we had a moment to speak, much less form a plan of attack, the lion rose, spat at us defiantly, and deliberately jumped off the crag. We heard him strike with a frightful thud.

Surprise held us dumb. To take the leap to the slope below seemed beyond any beast not endowed with wings. We saw the lion bounding down the identical trail which the other lion had taken. Jones came out of his momentary indecision.

"Hold the dogs! Call them back!" he yelled hoarsely. "They'll kill the lion we tied! They'll kill him!"

The hounds had scattered off the bench here and there, everywhere, to come together on the trail below. Already they were in full cry with the matchless Don at the fore. Manifestly to call them back was an injustice, as well as impossible. In ten seconds they were out of sight.

In silence we waited, each listening, each feeling the tragedy of the situation, each praying that they would pass by the poor, helpless, bound lion. Suddenly the regular baying swelled to a burst of savage, snarling fury, such as the pack made in a vicious fight. This ceased—short silence ensued; Don's sharp voice woke the echoes, then the regular baying continued.

As with one thought, we all sat down. Painful as

● ● ●

the certainty was, it was not so painful as that listening, hoping suspense.

"Shore they can't be blamed," said Jim finally. "Bumping their nose into a tied lion that way—how'd they know?"

"Who could guess the second lion would jump off that quick and run back to our captive?" burst out Jones.

"Shore we might have knowed it," replied Jim. "Well, I'm goin' after the pack."

He gathered up his lasso and strode off the bench. Jones said he would climb back to the rim, and I followed Jim.

Why the lions ran in that particular direction was clear to me when I saw the trail. It was a runway, smooth and hard packed. I trudged along it with rather less enjoyment than on any trail I had ever followed to the canyon. Jim waited for me over the cedar ridge and showed me where the captive lion lay dead. The hounds had not torn him. They had killed him and passed on after the other.

"He was a fine fellow, all of seven feet; we'll skin him on our way back."

Only dogged determination coupled with a sense of duty to the hounds kept us on that trail. For the time being enthusiasm had been submerged. But we had to follow the pack.

Jim, less weighted down and perhaps less discour-

● ● ●

aged, forged ahead up and down. The sun had burned all the morning coolness out of the air. I perspired and panted and began to grow weary. Jim's signal called me to hurry. I took to a trot and came upon him and the hounds under a small cedar. The lion stood among the dead branches. His sides were shaking convulsively and his short breaths could be plainly heard. He had the most blazing eyes and most untamed expression of any wild creature I have ever seen; and this amazed me, considering I had kept him on a crag for over an hour, and had come to look upon him as my own.

"What'll we do, Jim, now that we have him treed?"

"Shore we'll tie him up," declared Jim.

The lion stayed in the cedar long enough for me to photograph him twice, then he leaped down again and took to his back trail. We followed as fast as we could, soon to find that the hounds had put him up another cedar. From this he jumped down among the dogs, scattered them as if they had been so many leaves, and bounded up the slope out of sight.

I laid aside my rifle and camera and tried to keep up with Jim. The lion ran straight up the slope and treed again under the wall. Before we covered half the distance he was on the go once more, flying down in clouds of dust.

"Don is makin' him hump," said Jim.

● ● ●

And that alone was enough to spur us on. We would reward the noble hound if we had the staying power. Don and his pack ran westward this time, and along a mile of the beaten trail put him up two more trees. But these we could not see and judged only by the sound.

"Look there!" cried Jim. "Darn me if he ain't comin' right at us."

It was true. Ahead of us the lion appeared, loping wearily. We stopped in our tracks undecided. Jim drew his revolver. Once or twice the lion disappeared behind stones and cedars. When he sighted us he stopped, looked back, then again turning toward us, he left the trail to plunge down. He had barely gotten out of sight when old Don came pattering along the trail; then Ranger leading the others. Don did not even put his nose to the ground where the lion had switched, but leaped aside and went down. Here the long section of slope between the lion's runway and the second wall had been weathered and worn, racked and convulsed into deep ravines, with ridges between. We climbed and fell and toiled on, always with the bay of the hounds in our ears. We leaped fissures, we loosened avalanches, rolling them to crash and roar below, and send long, rumbling echoes out into the canyon.

A gorge in the yellow rock opened suddenly before us. We stood at the constricted neck of one of the

● ● ●

great splits in the second wall. The side opposite was almost perpendicular, and formed of mass on mass of broken stones. This was a weathered slope on a gigantic scale. Points of cliffs jutted out; caves and cracks lined the wall.

"This is a rough place," said Jim; "but a lion could get over the second wall here, an' I believe a man could too. The hounds seemed to be back further toward where the split narrows."

Through densely massed cedars and thickets of prickly thorns we wormed our way to come out at the neck of the gorge.

"There ye are!" sang out Jim. The hounds were all on a flat shelf some few feet below us, and on a sharp point of rock close by, but too far for the dogs to reach, crouched the lion. He was gasping and frothing at the mouth.

"Shore if he'd only stay there—" said Jim.

He loosened his lasso, and stationing himself just above the tired beast he prepared to cast down the loop. The first throw failed of its purpose, but the rope hit the lion. He got up painfully, it seemed, and faced the dogs. That way barred, he turned to the cliff. Almost opposite him a shelf leaned out. He looked at it, then paced to and fro like a beast in a cage.

He looked again at the hounds, then up at us, all around, and finally concentrated his attention on the

● ● ●

shelf; his long length sagged in the middle, he stretched low, his muscles gathered and strung, and he sprang like a tawny streak.

His aim was true, the whole fore part of his body landed on the shelf and he hung there. Then he slipped. We distinctly heard his claws scrape the hard, smooth rock. He fell, turning a somersault, struck twenty feet below on the rough slant, bounded from that to fall down, striking suddenly, and then to roll, a yellow wheel that lodged behind a rock and stretched out to move no more.

The hounds were silent; Jim and I were silent; a few little stones rattled, then were still. The dead silence of the canyon seemed to pay tribute to the lion's unquenchable spirit and to the freedom he had earned to the last.

8

How long Jim and I sat there we never knew. The second tragedy, not so pitiful but as heart sickening as the first, crushed our spirits.

"Shore he was a game lion," said Jim. "An' I'll have to get his skin."

"I'm all in, Jim. I couldn't climb out of that hole," I said.

"You needn't. Rest a little, take a good drink an' leave your canteen here for me; then get your things back there on the trail an' climb out. We're not far from West Point. I'll go back after the first lion's skin an' then climb straight up. You lead my horse to the point where you came off the rim."

He clattered along the gorge knocking the stones

● ● ●

and started down. I watched him letting himself over the end of the huge slabs until he passed out of my sight. A good, long drink revived me and I began the ascent.

From that moment on time did not matter to me. I forgot all about it. I felt only my leaden feet and my laboring chest and dripping skin. I did not even notice the additional weight of my rifle and camera, though they must have overburdened me. I kept my eyes on the lion runway and plunged away with short steps. To look at these towering walls would have been to surrender.

At last, stumbling, bursting, sick, I gained the rim and had to rest before I could mount. When I did get into the saddle I almost fell from it.

Jones and Emett were waiting for me at the promontory where I had tied my horse, and were soon acquainted with the particulars of my adventure, and that Jim would probably not get out for hours. We made tracks for camp, and never did a place rouse in me such a sense of gratefulness. Emett got dinner and left on the fire a kettle of potato stew for Jim. It was almost dark when that worthy came riding into camp. We never said a word as he threw the two lion skins on the ground.

"Fellows, you shore have missed the windup!" he exclaimed.

We all looked at him and he looked at us.

ROPING LIONS IN THE GRAND CANYON

● ● ●

"Was there any more?" I asked weakly.

"Shore! An' it beats hell! When I got the skin of the lion the dogs killed I started to work up to the place I knowed you'd leave my horse. It's bad climbing where you came down. I got on the side of that cliff an' saw where I could work out, if I could climb a smooth place. So I tried. There was little cracks an' ridges for my feet and hands. All to once, just above where I helped you down, I heard a growl. Looking up I saw a big lion, bigger'n any we chased except Sultan, an' he was pokin' his head out of a hole, an' shore telling me to come no further. I couldn't let go with either hand to reach my gun, because I'd have fallen, so I yelled at him with all my might. He spit at me an' then walked out of the hole over the bench as proud as a lord an' jumped down where I couldn't see him any more. I climbed out all right, but he'd gone. An' I'll tell you for a minute he shore made me sweat."

"By George!" I yelled, greatly excited. "I heard that lion breathing. Don chased him up there. I heard hard, wheezing breaths somewhere behind me, but in the excitement I didn't pay any attention to them. I thought it was Jones panting, but now I know what it meant."

"Shore. He was there all the time, lookin' at you an' maybe he could have reached you."

We were all too exhausted for more discussion,

● ● ●

and putting that off until the next day we sought our beds. It was hardly any wonder that I felt myself jumping even in my sleep, and started up wildly more than once in the dead of night.

Morning found us all rather subdued, yet more inclined to a philosophical resignation as regarded the difficulties of our special kind of hunting. Capturing the lions on the level of the plateau was easy compared to following them down into canyons and bringing them up alone. We all agreed that that was next to impossible. Another feature, which before we had not considered, added to our perplexity and it was a dawning consciousness that we would be perhaps less cruel if we killed the lions outright. Jones and Emett arrayed themselves on the side that life even in captivity was preferable; while Jim and I, no doubt still under the poignant influence of the last lion's heroic race and end, inclined to freedom or death. We compromised on the reasonable fact that as yet we had shown only a jackass kind of intelligence.

About eleven o'clock while the others had deserted camp temporarily for some reason or other, I was lounging upon an odorous bed of pine needles. The sun shone warmly, the sky gleamed bright azure through the openings of the great trees, a dry west breeze murmured through the forest. I was lying on my bed musing idly and watching a yellow woodpecker when suddenly I felt a severe bite on my

● ● ●

shoulder. I imagined an ant had bitten me through my shirt. In a moment or so afterward I received, this time on my breast, another bite that left no room for imagination. There was some kind of an animal inside my shirt, and one that made a mosquito, black-fly, or flea seem tame.

Suddenly a thought swept on the heels of my indolent and rather annoying realization. Could I have gotten from the Navajo what Jim and Jones so characteristically called " 'em"? I turned cold all over. And on the very instant I received another bite that burned like fire.

The return of my companions prevented any open demonstration of my fears and condition of mind, but I certainly swore inwardly. During the dinner hour I felt all the time as if I had on a horsehair shirt with the ends protruding toward my skin, and, in the exaggerated sensitiveness of the moment, made sure " 'em" were chasing up and down my back.

After dinner I sneaked off into the woods. I remembered that Emett had said there was only one way to get rid of " 'em," and that was to disrobe and make a microscopical search of garments and person. With serious mind and murderous intent I undressed. In the middle of the back of my jersey I discovered several long, uncanny, gray things.

"I guess I got 'em," I said gravely.

Then I sat on a pine log in a state of unadorned na-

● ● ●

ture, oblivious to all around, intent only on the massacre of the things that had violated me. How much time flew I could not guess. Great loud "Haw-haws!" roused me to consternation. There behind me stood Jones and Emett shaking as if with the ague.

"It's not funny!" I shouted in a rage. I had the unreasonable suspicion that they had followed me to see my humiliation. Jones, who cracked a smile about as often as the equinoxes came, and Emett, the sober Mormon, laughed until they cried.

"I was—just wondering—what your folks would—think—if they—saw you—now," gurgled Jones.

That brought to me the humor of the thing, and I joined in their mirth.

"All I hope is that you fellows will get ' 'em' too," I said.

"The good Lord preserve me from that particular breed of Navvy's," cried Emett. Jones wriggled all over at the mere suggestion. Now so much from the old plainsman, who had confessed to intimate relations with every creeping, crawling thing in the West, attested powerfully to the unforgettable singularity of what I got from Navvy.

I returned to camp determined to make the best of the situation, which, owing to my failure to catch all of the gray devils, remained practically unchanged. Jim had been acquainted with my dilemma, as was

● ● ●

manifest in his wet eyes and broad grin with which he greeted me.

"I think I'd scalp the Navvy," he said.

"You make the Indian sleep outside after this, snow or no snow," was Jones's suggestion.

"No, I won't; I won't show a yellow streak like that. Besides, I want to give 'em to you fellows."

A blank silence followed my statement, to which Jim replied:

"Shore that'll be easy; Jones'll have 'em, so'll Emett, an' by thunder I'm scratchin' now."

"Navvy, look here," I said, severely, "mucha no bueno! heap bad! You—me!" Here I scratched myself and made signs that a wooden Indian would have understood.

"Me savvy," he replied, sullenly, then flared up. "Heap big lie."

He turned with dignity, and walked away amid the roars of my gleeful comrades.

9

One by one my companions sought their blankets, leaving the shadows, the dying embers, the slow-rising moan of the night wind to me. Old Moze got up from among the other hounds and limped into my tent, where I heard him groan as he lay down. Don, Sounder and Ranger were fast asleep in well-earned rest. Shep, one of the pups, whined and impatiently tossed his short chain. Remembering that he had not been loose all day, I unbuckled his collar and let him go.

He licked my hand, stretched and shook himself, lifted his shapely, sleek head and sniffed the wind. He trotted around the circle cast by the fire and looked out into the darkening shadows. It was plain that Shep's instincts were developing fast; he was

● ● ●

ambitious to hunt. But sure in my belief that he was afraid of the black night and would stay in camp, I went to bed.

The Navajo who slept with me snored serenely and Moze growled in his dreams; the wind swept through the pines with an intermittent rush. Sometime in the after part of the night I heard a distant sound. Remote, mournful, wild, it sent a chill creeping over me. Borne faintly to my ears, it was a fit accompaniment to the moan of the wind in the pines. It was not the cry of a trailing wolf, nor the lonesome howl of a prowling coyote, nor the strange, low sound, like a cough, of a hunting cougar, though it had a semblance of all three. It was the bay of a hound, thinned out by distance, and it served to keep me wide awake. But for a while, what with the roar and swell of the wind and Navvy's snores, I could hear it only at long intervals.

Still, in the course of an hour, I followed the sound, or imagined so, from a point straight in line with my feet to one at right angles with my head. Finally deciding it came from Shep, and fancying he was trailing a deer or coyote, I tried to go to sleep again.

In this I would have succeeded had not, all at once, our captive lions begun to growl. That ominous, low murmuring awoke me with a vengeance, for it was unusual for them to growl in the middle of the night. I wondered if they, as well as the pup, had gotten the scent of a prowling lion.

● ● ●

I reached down to my feet and groped in the dark for Moze. Finding him, I gave him a shake. The old gladiator groaned, stirred, and came out of what must have been dreams of hunting meat. He slapped his tail against my bed. As luck would have it, just then the wind abated to a soft moan, and clear and sharp came the bay of a hound. Moze heard it, for he stopped wagging his tail, his body grew tense under my hand, and he vented his low, deep grumble.

I lay there undecided. To wake my companions was hardly to be considered, and to venture off into the forest alone, where old Sultan might be scouting, was not exactly to my taste. And trying to think what to do, and listening for the bay of the pup, and hearing mostly the lions growling and the wind roaring, I fell asleep.

"Hey! are you ever going to get up!" someone yelled into my drowsy brain. I roused and opened my eyes. The yellow, flickering shadows on the wall of my tent told me that the sun had long risen. I found my companions finishing breakfast. The first thing I did was to look over the dogs. Shep, the black-and-white pup, was missing.

"Where's Shep?" I asked.

"Shore I ain't seen him this mornin'," replied Jim.

Thereupon I told what I had heard during the night.

"Everybody listen," said Jones.

We quieted down and sat like statues. A gentle,

• • •

cool breeze, barely moving the pine tips, had succeeded the night wind. The sound of horses munch-
ing their oats, and an occasional clink, rattle, and
growl from the lions, did not drown the faint but unmistakable yelps of a pup.

"South, toward the canyon," said Jim, as Jones got
up.

"Now, it'd be funny if that little Shep, just to get
even with me for tying him up so often, has treed a
lion all by himself," commented Jones. "And I'll bet
that's just what he's done."

He called the hounds about him and hurried westward through the forest.

"Shore it might be." Jim shook his head knowingly. "I reckon it's only a rabbit, but anythin' might
happen in this place."

I finished breakfast and went into my tent for
something—I forget what, for wild yells from Emett
and Jim brought me flying out again.

"Listen to that!" cried Jim, pointing west.

The hounds had opened up; their full, wild chorus
floated clearly on the breeze, and above it Jones's
stentorian yell signaled us.

"Shore the old man can yell," continued Jim. "Grab
your lassos an' hump yourselves. I've got the collar
an' chain."

"Come on, Navvy," shouted Emett. He grasped the
Indian's wrist and started to run, jerking Navvy into the

● ● ●

air at every jump. I caught up my camera and followed. We crossed two shallow hollows, and then saw the hounds and Jones among the pines not far ahead.

In my excitement I outran my companions and dashed into an open glade. First I saw Jones waving his long arms; next the dogs, noses upward, and Don actually standing on his hind legs; then a dead pine with a well-known tawny shape outlined against the blue sky.

"Hurrah for Shep!" I yelled, and right vigorously did my comrades join in.

"It's another female," said Jones, when we calmed down, "and fair sized. That's the best tree for our purpose that I ever saw a lion in. So spread out, boys; surround her and keep noisy."

Navvy broke from Emett at this juncture and ran away. But evidently overcome by curiosity, he stopped to hide behind a bush, from which I saw his black head protruding.

When Jones swung himself on the first stubby branch of the pine, the lioness, some fifteen feet above, leaped to another limb, and the one she had left cracked, swayed, and broke. It fell directly upon Jones, the blunt end striking his head and knocking him out of the tree. Fortunately, he landed on his feet; otherwise there would surely have been bones broken. He appeared stunned, and reeled so that Emett caught him. The blood poured from a wound in his head.

This sudden shock sobered us instantly. On examina-

● ● ●

tion we found a long, jagged cut in Jones's scalp. We bathed it with water from my canteen and with snow Jim procured from a nearby hollow, eventually stopping the bleeding. I insisted on Jones coming to camp to have the wound properly dressed, and he insisted on having it bound with a bandana, after which he informed us that he was going to climb the tree again.

We objected to this. Each of us declared his willingness to go up and rope the lion; but Jones would not hear of it.

"I'm not doubting your courage," he said. "It's only that you cannot tell what move the lion would make next, and that's the danger."

We could not gainsay this, and as not one of us wanted to kill the animal or let her go, Jones had his way. So he went up the tree, passed the first branch and then another. The lioness changed her position, growled, spat, clawed the twigs, tried to keep the tree trunk between her and Jones, and at length got out on a branch in a most favorable position for roping.

The first cast of the lasso did the business, and Jim and Emett with nimble fingers tied up the hounds.

"Coming," shouted Jones. He slid down, hand over hand, on the rope, the lioness holding his weight with apparent ease.

"Make your noose ready," he yelled to Emett.

I had to drop my camera to help Jones and Jim pull the animal from her perch. The branches broke

● ● ●

in a shower; then the lioness, hissing, snarling, whirling, plunged down. She nearly jerked the rope out of our hands, but we lowered her to Emett, who noosed her hind paws in a flash.

"Make fast your rope," shouted Jones. "There, that's good! Now let her down—easy."

As soon as the lioness touched ground we let go the lasso, which whipped up and over the branch. She became a round, yellow, rapidly moving ball. Emett was the first to catch the loose lasso, and he checked the rolling cougar. Jones leaped to assist him and the two of them straightened out the struggling animal, while Jim swung another noose at her. On the second throw he caught a front paw.

"Pull hard! Stretch her out!" yelled Jones. He grasped a stout piece of wood and pushed it at the lioness. She caught it in her mouth, making the splinters fly. Jones shoved her head back on the ground and pressed his brawny knee on the bar of wood.

"The collar! The collar! Quick!" he called.

I threw chain and collar to him, which in a moment he had buckled round her neck.

"There, we've got her!" he said. "It's only a short way over to camp, so we'll drag her without muzzling."

As he rose the lioness lurched and, reaching him, fastened her fangs in his leg. Jones roared. Emett and Jim yelled. And I, though frightened, was so ob-

● ● ●

sessed with the idea of getting a picture that I began to fumble with the shutter of my camera.

"Grab the chain! Pull her off!" bawled Jones.

I ran in, took up the chain with both hands, and tugged with all my might. Emett, too, had all his weight on the lasso round her neck. Between the two of us we choked her hold loose, but she brought Jones's leather legging in her teeth. Then I dropped the chain and jumped.

"**___ ___**___ ___!" exploded Jones to me. "Do you think more of a picture than of saving my life?" Having expressed this not unreasonable protest, he untied the lasso that Emett had made fast to a small sapling.

Then the three men, forming points of a triangle around an animated center, began a march through the forest that for variety of action and splendid vociferation beat any show I ever beheld.

So rare was it that the Navajo came out of his retreat and, straightway forgetting his reverence and fear, began to execute a ghost dance, or a war dance, or at any rate some kind of an Indian dance, along the sidelines.

There were moments when the lioness had Jim and Jones on the ground and Emett wobbling; others when she ran on her bound legs and chased the two in front and dragged the one behind; others when she came within an ace of getting her teeth in somebody.

ROPING LIONS IN THE GRAND CANYON

● ● ●

They had caught a Tartar. They dared not let her go, and though Jones evidently ordered it, no one made fast his rope to a tree. There was no opportunity. She was in the air three parts of the time, and the fourth she was invisible for dust. The lassos were each thirty feet long, but even with that the men could just barely keep out of her reach.

Then came the climax, as it always comes in a lion hunt, unerringly, unexpectedly, and with lightning swiftness. The three men were nearing the bottom of the second hollow, well spread out, lassos taut, facing one another. Jones stumbled and the lioness leaped his way. The weight of both brought Jim over, sliding and slipping, with his rope slackening. The leap of the lioness carried her within reach of Jones; and as he raised himself, back toward her, she reached a big paw for him just as Emett threw all his bull strength and bulk on his lasso.

The seat of Jones's trousers came away with the lioness's claws. Then she fell backward, overcome by Emett's desperate lunge. Jones sprang up with the velocity of an Arab tumbler, and his scarlet face, working spasmodically, and his moving lips, showed how utterly unable he was to give expression to his rage. I had a stitch in my side that nearly killed me, but laugh I had to, though I should die for it.

No laughing matter was it for them. They volleyed and thundered back and forth meaningless words of

● ● ●

which "hell" was the only one distinguishable, and probably the word that best described their situation.

All the while, however, they had been running from the lioness, which brought them, before they realized it, right into camp. Our captive lions cut up fearfully at the hubbub, and the horses stampeded in terror.

"Whoa!" yelled Jones, whether to his companions or to the struggling cougar no one knew. But Navvy thought Jones addressed the cougar.

"Whoa!" repeated Navvy. "No savvy whoa! No savvy whoa!" which proved conclusively that the Navajo had understanding as well as wit.

Soon we had another captive safely chained and growling away in tune with the others. I went back to untie the hounds, to find them sulky and out of sorts from being so unceremoniously treated. They noisily trailed the lioness into camp, where, finding her chained, they formed a ring around her.

Thereafter the day passed in round-the-campfire chat and task. For once Jim looked at Navvy with toleration. We dressed the wound in Jones's head and laughed at the condition of his trousers and at his awkward attempts to piece them.

"Mucha dam' cougie," remarked Navvy. "No savvy whoa!"

The lions growled all day. And Jones kept repeating, "To think how Shep fooled me!"

10

Next morning Jones was out bright and early, yelling at Navvy to hurry with the horses, calling to the hounds and lions, just as usual.

Navvy had finally come to his full share of praise from all of us. Even Jim acknowledged that the Indian was invaluable to a hunting party in a country where grass and water were hard to find and wild horses haunted the trails.

"*Tohodena! Tohodena!* (Hurry! Hurry!)" said Navvy, mimicking Jones that morning.

As we sat down to breakfast he loped off into the forest, and before we got up the bells of the horses were jingling in the hollow.

ROPING LIONS IN THE GRAND CANYON

● ● ●

"I believe it's going to be cloudy," said Jones, "and if so we can hunt all day."

We rode down the ridge to the left of Middle Canyon, and had trouble with the hounds all the way. First they ran foul of a coyote, which was the one and only beast they could not resist. Spreading out to head them off, we separated. I cut into a hollow and rode to its head, where I went up. I heard the hounds and presently saw a big, white coyote making fast time through the forest glades. It looked as if he would cross close in front of me, so I pulled Foxie to a standstill, jumped off and knelt with my rifle ready. But the sharp-eyed coyote saw my horse and shied off. I had not much hope to hit him so far away, and the five bullets I sent after him, singing and zipping, served only to make him run faster. I mounted Foxie and intercepted the hounds coming up sharply on the trail, and turned them toward my companions, now hallooing from the ridge below.

Then the pack lost a good hour on several lion tracks that were a day old, and for such trails we had no time. We reached the cedars, however, at seven o'clock, and as the sky was overcast with low dun-colored clouds and the air cool, we were sure it was not too late.

One of the capes of the plateau between Middle and Left Canyon was a narrow strip of rock, covered with a dense cedar growth and cut up into smaller

● ● ●

canyons, all running down inevitably toward the great canyon. With but a single bark to warn us, Don got out of our sight and hearing; and while we split to look and call for him the remainder of the pack found the lion trail that he had gone on, and they left us trying to find a way out as well as to find each other. I kept the hounds in hearing for some time and meanwhile I signaled to Emett, who was on my right flank. Jones and Jim might as well have vanished off the globe for all I could see or hear of them. A deep, narrow gully into which I had to lead Foxie and carefully coax him out took so much time that when I once more reached a level I could not hear the hounds or get an answer to my signal cry.

"Waa-hoo!" I called again.

Away on the dry rarefied air pealed the cry, piercing the cedar forest, splitting sharp in the vaulted canyons, rolling loud and long, to lose power, to die away in muffling echo. But the silence returned no answer.

I rode on under the cedars, through a dark, gloomy forest, silent, almost spectral, which brought irresistibly to my mind the words, "I found me in a gloomy wood astray." I was lost, though I knew the direction of the camp. This section of cedar forest was all but impenetrable. Dead cedars were massed in gray tangles; live cedars, branches touching the ground, grew close together. In this labyrinth I lost my bearings. I

● ● ●

turned and turned, crossed my own back trail, which in desperation I followed, coming out of the cedars at the deep and narrow canyon.

Here I fired my revolver. The echo boomed out like the report of heavy artillery, but no answering shot rewarded me. There was no alternative save to wander along the canyon and through the cedars until I found my companions. This I began to do, disgusted with my awkwardness in losing them. Turning Foxie westward, I had scarcely gotten under way when Don came trotting toward me.

"Hello, old boy!" I called. Don appeared as happy to see me as I was to see him. He flopped down on the ground; his dripping tongue rolled as he panted; covered with dust and flecked with light froth, he surely looked to be a tired hound.

"All in, eh, Don!" I said, dismounting. "Well, we'll rest awhile." Then I discovered blood on his nose, which I found to have come from a deep scratch. "A—ah! been pushing a lion too hard this morning? Got your nose scratched, didn't you? You great, crazy hound, don't you know some day you'll chase your last lion?"

Don wagged his tail as if to say he knew it all very well. I wet my handkerchief from my canteen and started to wash the blood and dust from his nose, when he whined and licked my fingers.

"Thirsty?" I asked, sitting down beside him. Dent-

● ● ●

ing the top of my hat, I poured in as much water as it would hold and gave him to drink. Four times he emptied my improvised cup before he was satisfied. Then with a sigh of relief he lay down again.

The three of us rested there for perhaps half an hour, Don and I sitting quietly on the wall of the canyon, while Foxie browsed on occasional tufts of grass. During that time the hound never raised his sleek, dark head, which showed conclusively the nature of the silence. And now that I had company—as good company as any hunter ever had—I was once more contented.

Don got up, at length, of his own volition and with a wag of his tail set off westward along the rim. Remounting my mustang, I kept as close to Don's heels as the rough going permitted. The hound, however, showed no disposition to hurry, and I let him have his way without a word.

We came out in the notch of the great amphitheater or curve we had named the Bay, and I saw again the downward slope, the bold steps, the color and depth below.

I was just about to yell a signal cry when I saw Don, with hair rising stiff, run forward. He took a dozen jumps, then yelping, broke down the steep, yellow and green gorge. He disappeared before I knew what had happened.

Shortly I found a lion track, freshly made, leading

● ● ●

down. I believed I could follow wherever Don led, so I decided to go after him. I tied Foxie securely, removed my coat, kicked off spurs and chaps, and remembering past unnecessary toil, fastened a red bandana to the top of a dead snag to show me where to come up on my way out. Then I carefully strapped my canteen and camera on my back, made doubly secure my revolver, put on my heavy gloves, and started down. And I realized at once that only so lightly encumbered should I have ever ventured down the slope.

Little benches of rock, grassy on top, with here and there cedar trees, led steeply down for perhaps five hundred feet. A precipice stopped me. From it I heard Don baying below, and almost instantly saw the yellow gleam of a lion in a treetop.

"Hi! Hi! Hi! Hi! Hi!" I yelled in wild encouragement.

I felt it would be wise to look before I leaped. The Bay lay under me, a mile wide where it opened into the great slumbering smoky canyon. All below was chaos of splintered stone and slope, green jumble of cedar, ruined, detached, sliding, standing cliff walls, leaning yellow crags—an awful hole. But I could get down, and that was all I cared for. I ran along to the left, jumping cracks, bounding over the uneven stones with sure, swift feet, and came to where the cliff ended in weathered slope and scaly bench.

ROPING LIONS IN THE GRAND CANYON

● ● ●

It was like a game, going down that canyon. My heavy nailed boots struck fire from the rocks. My heavy gloves protected my hands as I slid and hung on and let go. I outfooted the avalanches, and wherever I came to a scaly slope or bank or decayed rock, I leaped down in sheer delight.

But all too soon my progress was barred; once under the cliff I found only a gradual slope and many obstacles to go round or surmount. Luck favored me, for I ran across a runway and, keeping to it, made better time. I heard Don long before I tried to see him, and yelled at intervals to let him know I was coming. A white bank of weathered stones led down to a clump of cedars from where Don's bay came spurring me to greater efforts. I flew down this bank, and through an opening saw the hound standing with fore feet against a cedar. The branches over him swayed, and I saw an indistinct, tawny form move downward in the air. Then succeeded the crash and rattle of stones. Don left the tree and disappeared.

I dashed down, dodged under the cedars, threaded a maze of rocks, to find myself in a ravine with a bare, water-worn floor. In patches of sand showed the fresh tracks of Don and the lion. Running down this dry, clean bed was the easiest going I ever found in the canyon. Every rod the course jumped in a fall from four to ten feet, often more, and these I slid

● ● ●

down. How I ever kept Don in hearing was a marvel, but still I did.

The lion evidently had no further intention of taking to a tree. From the size of his track I concluded he was old, and I feared every moment to hear the sounds of a fight. Jones had said that nearly always in the case of one hound chasing an old lion, the lion would lie in wait for him and kill him. And I was afraid for Don.

Down, down, down, we went, till the yellow rim above seemed a thin band of gold. I saw that we were almost to the canyon proper, and I wondered what would happen when we reached it. The dark shaded watercourse suddenly shot out into bright light and ended in a deep cove, with perpendicular walls fifty feet high. I could see where a few rods farther on this cove opened into a huge, airy, colored canyon.

I called the hound, wondering if he had gone to the right or left of the cove. His bay answered me coming from the cedars far to the right. I turned with all the speed left in me, for I felt the chase nearing an end. Tracks of hound and lion once more showed in the dust. The slope was steep and stones I sent rolling cracked down below. Soon I had a cliff above me and had to go slow and cautiously. A misstep or slide would have precipitated me into the cove.

Almost before I knew what I was about, I stood gasping on the gigantic second wall of the canyon,

● ● ●

with nothing but thin air under me, except, far below, faint and indistinct purple clefts, red ridges, dotted slopes, running down to merge in a dark, winding strip of water that was the Rio Colorado. A sullen murmur soared out of the abyss.

The coloring of my mood changed. Never had the canyon struck me so terribly with its illimitable space, its dread depth, its unscalable cliffs, and particularly with the desolate, forbidding quality of its silence.

I heard Don bark. Turning the corner of the cliff wall, I saw him on a narrow shelf. He was coming toward me and when he reached me he faced again to the wall and barked fiercely. The hair on his neck bristled. I knew he did not fancy that narrow strip of rock, nor did I. But a sudden, grim, cold something had taken possession of me, and I stepped forward.

"Come on, Don, old fellow, we've got him corralled."

That was the first instance I ever knew of Don's hesitation in the chase of a lion. I had to coax him to me. But once started, he took the lead and I closely followed.

The shelf was twenty feet wide and upon it close to the wall, in the dust, were the deep imprints of the lion. A jutting corner of cliff wall hid my view. I peeped around it. The shelf narrowed on the other side to a yard in width, and climbed gradually by

● ● ●

broken steps. Don passed the corner, looked back to see if I was coming and went on. He did this four times, once even stopping to wait for me.

"I'm with you, Don!" I grimly muttered. "We'll see this trail out to a finish."

I had now no eyes for the wonders of the place, though I could not but see, as I bent a piercing gaze ahead, the ponderous overhanging wall above, and sense the bottomless depth below. I felt rather than saw the canyon swallows, sweeping by in darting flight, with soft rustle of wings, and I heard the shrill chirp of some strange cliff inhabitant.

Don ceased barking. How strange that seemed to me! We were no longer man and hound, but companions, brothers, each one relying on the other. A protruding corner shut us from sight of what was beyond. Don slipped around. I had to go sidewise, and shuddered as my fingers bit into the wall.

To my surprise I soon found myself on the floor of a shallow wind cave. The lion trail led straight across it and on. Shelves of rock stuck out above, under which I hurriedly walked. I came upon a shrub cedar growing in a niche and marveled to see it there. Don went slower and slower.

We suddenly rounded a point, to see the lion lying in a boxlike space in the wall. The shelf ended there. I had once before been confronted with a like situation, and had expected to find it here, so was not

• • •

frightened. The lion looked up from his task of licking a bloody paw and uttered a fierce growl. His tail
began to lash to and fro; it knocked the little stones
off the shelf. I heard them click on the wall. Again
and again he spat, showing great, white fangs. He
was a Tom, heavy and large.

It had been my purpose, of course, to photograph
this lion, and, now that we had cornered him, I pro-
posed to do it. What would follow had only hazily
formed in my mind, but the nucleus of it was that he
should go free. I got my camera, opened it, and focused from between twenty and twenty-five feet.

Then a growl from Don and roar from the lion
bade me come to my senses. I did so, and my first
movement after seeing the lion had risen threaten-
ingly was to whip out my revolver.

The lion's cruel yellow eyes darkened and darkened. In an instant I saw my error. Jones had always
said in case any one of us had to face a lion, never
for a single instant to shift his glance. I had forgotten
that, and in that short interval when I focused my
camera the lion had seen I meant him no harm, or
feared him, and he had risen. Even then in desperate
lessening ambition for a great picture I attempted to
take one, still keeping my glance on him.

It was then that the appalling nature of my predicament made itself plain to me. The lion leaped ten
feet and stood snarling horribly right in my face.

ROPING LIONS IN THE GRAND CANYON

● ● ●

Brave, noble Don, with infinitely more sense and courage than I possessed, faced the lion and bayed him in his teeth. I raised the revolver and aimed twice, each time lowering it because I feared to shoot in such a precarious position. To wound the lion would be the worst thing I could do, and I knew that only a shot through the brain would kill him in his tracks.

"Hold him, Don, hold him!" I yelled, and I took a backward step. The lion put forward one big paw, his eyes now all purple blaze. I backed again and he came forward. Don gave ground slowly. Once the lion flashed a yellow paw at him. It was frightful to see the widespread claws.

In the consternation of the moment I allowed the lion to back me across the front of the wind cave, where I saw, the moment it was too late, I should have taken advantage of more space to shoot him.

Fright succeeded consternation, and I began to tremble. The lion was master of the situation. What would happen when I came to the narrow point on the shelf where it would be impossible for me to back around? I almost fainted. The thought of heroic Don saved me, and the weak moment passed.

"By God, Don, you've got the nerve, and I must have it too!"

I stopped in my tracks. The lion, appearing huge now, took slow catlike steps toward me, backing Don

● ● ●

almost against my knees. He was so close I smelled him. His wonderful eyes, clear blue fire circled by yellow flame, fascinated me. Hugging the wall with my body, I brought the revolver up, short armed, and with clenched teeth, and nerve strained to the breaking point, I aimed between the eyes and pulled the trigger.

The left eye seemed to go out blankly, then followed the bellow of the revolver and the smell of powder. The lion uttered a sound that was a mingling of snarls, howls and roars, and he rose straight up, towering high over my head, beating the wall heavily with his paws.

In helpless terror I stood there, forgetting my weapon, fearing only the beast would fall over on me.

But in death agony he bounded out from the wall to fall into space.

I sank down on the shelf, legs powerless, body in cold sweat. As I waited, slowly my mind freed itself from a tight iron band and a sickening relief filled my soul. Tensely I waited and listened. Don whined once.

Would the lion never strike? What seemed a long period of time ended in a low, distant roar of sliding rock, quickly dying into the solemn stillness of the canyon.

11

I lay there for some moments, slowly recovering, eyes on the far-distant escarpment, now darkly red and repellent to me. When I got up my legs were still shaky and I had the strange, weak sensation of a long bedridden invalid. Three attempts were necessary before I could trust myself on the narrow strip of shelf. But once around it, with the peril passed, I braced up and soon reached the turn in the wall.

After that the ascent out of the Bay was only a matter of work, which I gave with a will. Don did not evince any desire for more hunting that day. We reached the rim together, and after a short rest I mounted my horse, and we turned for camp.

The sun had long slanted toward the western hori-

● ● ●

zon when I saw the blue smoke of our campfire among the pines. The hounds rose up and barked as Don trotted in to the blaze, and my companions, just sitting to dinner, gave me a noisy greeting.

"Shore we'd began to get worried," said Jim. "We all had it comin' to us today, and don't you forget that."

Dinner lasted for a long hour. Besides being half famished we all took time between bites to talk. I told my story first, expecting my friends to be overwhelmed, but they were not.

"It's been the greatest day of lion hunting that I ever experienced," declared Jones. "We ran bang into a nest of lions and they split. We all split and the hounds split. That tells the tale. We have nothing to show for our day's toil. Six lions chased, rounded up, treed, holed, and one lion killed, and we haven't even his skin to show. I did not go down, but I helped Ranger and two of the pups chase a lion all over the lower end of the plateau. We treed him twice and I yelled for you fellows till my voice was gone."

"Well," said Emett, "I fell in with Sounder and Jude. They were hot on a trail which in a mile or two turned up this way. I came on them just at the edge of the pines, where they had treed their game. I sat under that pine tree for five hours, fired all my shots to make you fellows come, yelled myself hoarse and then tried to tie up the lion alone. He jumped out and

● ● ●

ran over the rim, where neither I nor the dogs could follow."

"Shore I win, three of a kind," drawled Jim, as he got his pipe and carefully dusted the bowl. "When the stampede came, I got my hands on Moze and held him. I held Moze because just as the other hounds broke loose over to my right, I saw down into a little pocket where a fresh-killed deer lay half eaten. So I went down. I found two other carcasses layin' there, fresh killed last night, flesh all gone, hide gone, bones crushed, skull split open. An' damn me, fellows, if that little pocket wasn't all torn to pieces. The sage was crushed flat. The ground dug up, dead snags broken, and blood and hair everywhere. Lion tracks like leaves, and old Sultan's was there. I let Moze loose and he humped the trail of several lions south over the rim. Major got down first an' came back with his tail between his legs. Moze went down and I kept close to him. It wasn't far down, but steep and rocky, full of holes. Moze took the trail to a dark cave. I saw the tracks of three lions goin' in. Then I collared Moze an' waited for you fellows. I waited there all day, an' nobody came to my call. Then I made for camp."

"How do you account for the torn-up appearance of the place where you found the carcasses?" I asked.

"Lion fight, sure," replied Jones. "Maybe old Sultan ran across the three lions feeding, and pitched

● ● ●

into them. Such fights were common among the lions in Yellowstone Park when I was there."

"What chance have we to find those three lions in a cave where Jim chased them?"

"We stand a good chance," said Jones. "Especially if it storms tonight."

"Shore the snowstorm is comin'," returned Jim.

Darkness clapped down on us suddenly, and the wind roared in the pines like a mighty river tearing its way down a rocky pass. As we could not control the campfire, sparks of which blew fiercely, we extinguished it and went to bed. I had just settled myself comfortably to be sung to sleep by the concert in the pines, when Jones hailed me.

"Say, what do you think?" he yelled, when I had answered him. "Emett is mad. He's scratching to beat the band. He's got 'em."

I signaled his information with a loud whoop of victory.

"You're next, Jones! They're coming to you!"

I heard him grumble over my happy anticipation. Jim laughed and so did the Navajo, which made me suspect that he could understand more English than he wanted us to suppose.

Next morning a merry yell disturbed my slumbers. "Snowed in—snowed in!"

"Mucha snow—discass—no cougie—dam' no bueno!" exclaimed Navvy.

ROPING LIONS IN THE GRAND CANYON

● ● ●

When I peeped out to see the forest in the throes of a blinding blizzard, the great pines only pale, grotesque shadows, everything white mantled in a foot of snow, I emphasized the Indian words in straight English.

"Much snow—cold—no cougar—bad!"

"Stay in bed," yelled Jones.

"All right," I replied. "Say, Jones, have you got 'em yet?"

He vouchsafed me no answer. I went to sleep then and dozed off and on till noon, when the storm abated. We had dinner, or rather breakfast, round a blazing bonfire.

"It's going to clear up," said Jim.

The forest around us was a somber and gloomy place. The cloud that had enveloped the plateau lifted and began to move. It hit the treetops, sometimes rolling almost to the ground, then rising above the trees. At first it moved slowly, rolling, forming, expanding, blooming like a column of whirling gray smoke; then it gathered headway and rolled onward through the forest. A gray, gloomy curtain, moving and rippling, split by the trees, seemed to be passing over us. It rose higher and higher, to split up in great globes, to roll apart, showing glimpses of blue sky.

Shafts of golden sunshine shot down from these rifts, dispelling the shadows and gloom, moving in

115

● ● ●

paths of gold through the forest glade, gleaming with brilliantly colored fire from the snow-wreathed pines.

The cloud rolled away and the sun shone hot. The trees began to drip. A mist of diamonds filled the air, rainbows curved through every glade and feathered patches of snow floated down.

A great bank of snow, sliding from the pine over-head, almost buried the Navajo, to our infinite de-light. We all sought the shelter of the tents, and sleep again claimed us.

I awoke about five o'clock. The sun was low, mak-ing crimson paths in the white aisles of the forest. A cold wind promised a frosty morning.

"Tomorrow will be the day for lions," exclaimed Jones.

While we hugged the fire, Navvy brought up the horses and gave them their oats. The hounds sought their shelter and the lions lay hidden in their beds of pine. The round red sun dropped out of sight beyond the trees, a pink glow suffused all the ridges; blue shadows gathered in the hollow, shaded purple and stole upward. A brief twilight succeeded to a dark, coldly starlit night.

Once again, when I had crawled into the warm hole of my sleeping bag, was I hailed from the other tent.

Emett called me twice, and as I answered I heard Jones remonstrating in a low voice.

● ● ●

"Shore Jones has got 'em!" yelled Jim. "He can't keep it a secret no longer."

"Hey, Jones," I cried, "do you remember laughing at me?"

"No, I don't," growled Jones.

"Listen to this: Haw-haw! Haw! Haw! Ho-ho! Ho-ho! Bueno! Bueno!" and I wound up with a string of "Hi! Hi! Hi! Hi! Hi!"

The hounds rose up in a body and began to yelp.

"Lie down, pups," I called to them. "Nothing doing for you. It's only Jones has got 'em."

12

When we trooped out of the pines next morning, the sun, rising gloriously bright, had already taken off the keen edge of the frosty air, presaging a warm day. The white ridges glistened; the bunches of sage scintillated, and the cedars, tipped in snow, resembled trees with brilliant blossoms.

We lost no time riding for the mouth of Left Canyon, into which Jim had trailed the three lions. On the way the snow, as we had expected, began to thin out, and it failed altogether under the cedars, though there was enough on the branches to give us a drenching.

Jim reined in on the verge of a narrow gorge, and informed us the cave was below. Jones looked the

● ● ●

ground over and said Jim had better take the hounds down while the rest of us remained above to await developments.

Jim went down on foot, calling the hounds and holding them close. We listened eagerly for him to yell or the pack to open up, but we were disappointed. In less than half an hour Jim came climbing out, with the information that the lions had left the cave, probably the evening after he had chased them there.

"Well, then," said Jones, "let's split the pack, and hunt round the rims of these canyons. We can signal to each other if necessary."

So we arranged for Jim to take Ranger and the pups across Left Canyon; Emett to try Middle Canyon with Don and Moze; and we were to perform a like office in Right Canyon with Sounder and Jude. Emett rode back with us, leaving us where we crossed Middle Canyon.

Jones and I rimmed a mile of our canyon and worked out almost to the west end of the Bay, without finding so much as a single track, so we started to retrace our way. The sun was now hot; the snow all gone; the ground dry as if it had never been damp; and Jones grumbled that no success would attend our efforts this morning.

We reached the ragged mouth of Right Canyon, where it opened into the deep, wide Bay, and because

● ● ●

we hoped to hear our companions across the canyon, we rode close to the rim. Sounder and Jude both began to bark on a cliff; however, as we could find no tracks in the dust we called them off. Sounder obeyed reluctantly, but Jude wanted to get down over the wall.

"They scent a lion," averred Jones. "Let's put them over the wall."

Once permitted to go, the hounds needed no assistance. They ran up and down the rim till they found a crack. Hardly had they gone out of sight when we heard them yelping. We rushed to the rim and looked over. The first step was short, a crumbled section of wall, and from it led down a long slope, dotted here and there with cedars. Both hounds were baying furiously.

I spied Jude with her paws up on a cedar, and above her hung a lion, so close that she could nearly reach him. Sounder was not yet in sight.

"There! There!" I cried, directing Jones's glance. "Are we not lucky?"

"I see. By George! Come, we'll go down. Leave everything that you don't absolutely need."

Spurs, chaps, gun, coat, hat, I left on the rim, taking only my camera and lasso. I had forgotten to bring my canteen. We descended a ladder of shaley cliff, the steps of which broke under our feet. The slope below us was easy, and soon we stood on a

• • •

level with the lion. The cedar was small and afforded no good place for him. Evidently he jumped from the slope to the tree, and had hung where he first alighted.

"Where's Sounder? Look for him. I hear him below. This lion won't stay treed long."

I, too, heard Sounder. The cedar tree obstructed my view, and I moved aside. A hundred feet farther down the hound bayed under a tall piñon. High in the branches I saw a great mass of yellow, and at first glance thought Sounder had treed old Sultan. How I yelled! Then a second glance showed two lions close together.

"Two more! two more! look! look!" I yelled to Jones.

"Hi! Hi! Hi!" he joined his robust yell to mine, and for a moment we made the canyon bellow. When we stopped for breath the echoes bayed at us from the opposite walls.

"Waa-hoo!" Emett's signal, faint, far away, soaring but unmistakable, floated down to us. Across the jutting capes separating the mouths of these canyons, high above them on the rim wall of the opposite side of the Bay, stood a giant white horse silhouetted against the white sky. They made a brave picture, one most welcome to us. We yelled in chorus: "Three lions treed! Three lions treed! Come down—hurry!"

A crash of rolling stones made us wheel. Jude's

● ● ●

lion had jumped. He ran straight down, drawing Sounder from his guard. Jude went tearing after them.

"I'll follow; you stay here. Keep them up there, if you can!" yelled Jones. Then in long strides he passed down out of sight among the trees and crags.

It had all happened so quickly that I could scarcely realize it. The yelping of the hounds, the clattering of stones, grew fainter, telling me Jude and Sounder, with Jones, were going to the bottom of the Bay.

Both lions snarling at me brought me to a keen appreciation of the facts in the case. Two full-grown lions to be kept treed without hounds, without a companion, without a gun.

"This is fine! This is funny!" I cried, and for a moment I wanted to run. But the same grim, deadly feeling that had taken me with Don around the narrow shelf now rose in me stronger and fiercer. I pronounced one savage malediction upon myself for leaving my gun. I could not go for it; I would have to make the best of my error, and in the wildness born of the moment I swore if the lions would stay treed for the hounds they would stay treed for me.

First I photographed them from different positions; then I took up my stand about on a level with them in an open place on the slope where they had me in plain sight. I might have been fifty feet from them. They showed no inclination to come down.

ROPING LIONS IN THE GRAND CANYON

• • •

About this moment I heard hounds below, coming down from the left. I called and called, but they passed on down the canyon bottom in the direction Jones had taken.

Presently a chorus of bays, emphasized by Jones's yell, told me his lion had treed again.

"Waa-hoo!" rolled down from above.

I saw Emett farther to the left from the point where he had just appeared.

"Where—can—I—get—down?"

I surveyed the walls of the Bay. Cliff on cliff, slide on slide, jumble, crag, and ruin baffled my gaze. But I finally picked out a path.

"Farther to the left," I yelled, and waited. He passed on, Don at his heels.

"There," I yelled again, "stop there; let Don go down with your lasso, and come yourself."

I watched him swing the hound down a wall, and pull the slip noose free. Don slid to the edge of a slope, trotted to the right and left of crags, threaded the narrow places, and turned in the direction of the baying hounds. He passed on the verge of precipices that made me tremble for him; but surefooted as a goat, he went on safely down, to disappear far to my right.

Then I saw Emett sliding, leg wrapped around his lasso, down the first step of the rim. His lasso, doubled so as to reach round a cedar above, was too

● ● ●

short to extend to the landing below. He dropped, raising a cloud of dust and starting the stones. Pulling one end of his lasso up around the cedar, he gathered it in a coil on his arm and faced forward, following Don's trail.

What strides he took! In the clear light, with that wild red and yellow background, with the stones and gravel roaring down, streaming over the walls like waterfalls, he seemed a giant pursuing a foe. From time to time he sent up a yell of encouragement that wound down the canyon, to be answered by Jones and the baying hounds and then the strange echoes. At last he passed out of sight behind the crests of the trees; I heard him going down, down till the sounds came up faint and hollow.

I was left absolutely alone with my two lions and never did a hunter so delight in a situation. I sat there in the sun watching them. For a long time they were quiet, listening. But as the bays and yells below diminished in volume and occurrence and then ceased altogether, they became restless. It was then that I, remembering the lion I had held on top of the crag, began to bark like a hound. The lions became quiet once more.

I bayed them for an hour. My voice grew from hoarse to hoarser, and finally failed in my throat. The lions immediately grew restless again. The lower one hissed, spat and growled at me, and made many at-

● ● ●

tempts to start down, each one of which I frustrated by throwing stones under the tree. At length he made one more determined effort, turned head downward, and stepped from branch to branch.

I dashed down the incline with a stone in one hand and a long club in the other. Instinctively I knew I must hurt him—make him fear me. If he got far enough down to jump, he would either escape or have me helpless. I aimed deliberately at him, and hit him square in the ribs. He exploded in a spit-roar that raised my hair. Directly under him I wielded my club, pounded on the tree, thrashed at the branches and, like the crazy fool that I was, yelled at him:

"Go back! Go back! Don't you dare come down! I'd break your old head for you!"

Foolish or not, this means effectually stopped the descent. He climbed to his first perch. It was then, realizing what I had done, that I would certainly have made tracks from under the piñon, if I had not heard the faint yelp of a hound.

I listened. It came again, faint but clearer. I looked up at my lions. They too heard, for they were very still. I saw how strained they held their heads. I backed a little way up the slope. Then the faint yelp floated up again in the silence. Such dead, strange silence, that seemed never to have been broken! I saw the lions quiver, and if I ever heard anything in my life I heard their hearts thump. The yelp wafted up

● ● ●

again, closer this time. I recognized it; it belonged to Don. The great hound on the back trail of the other lion was coming to my rescue.

"It's Don! It's Don! It's Don!" I cried, shaking my club at the lions. "It's all up with you now!" What feelings stirred me then! Pity for those lions dominated me. Big, tawny, cruel fellows as they were, they shivered with fright. Their sides trembled. But pity did not hold me long; Don's yelp, now getting clear and sharp, brought back the rush of savage, grim sensations.

A full-toned bay attracted my attention from the lions to the downward slope. I saw a yellow form moving under the trees and climbing fast. It was Don.

"Hi! Hi! old boy!" I yelled.

Then it seemed he moved up like a shot and stood all his long length, fore paws against the piñon, his deep bay ringing defiance to the lions.

It was a great relief, not to say a probable necessity, for me to sit down just then.

"Now come down," I said to my lions; "you can't catch that hound, and you can't get away from him."

Moments passed. I was just on the point of deciding to go down to hurry up my comrades, when I heard the other hounds coming. Yelp on yelp, bay on bay, made welcome music to my ears. Then a black and yellow, swiftly flying string of hounds bore into

● ● ●

sight down the slope, streaked up and circled the piñon.

Jones, who at last showed his tall stooping form on the steep ascent, seemed as long in coming as the hounds had been swift.

"Did you get the lion? Where's Emett?" I asked in breathless eagerness.

"Lion tied—all fast," replied the panting Jones. "Left Emett—to guard—him."

"What are we to do now?"

"Wait—till I get my breath. Think out—a plan. We can't get both lions—out of one tree."

"All right," I replied, after a moment's thought. "I'll tie Sounder and Moze. You go up the tree. That first lion will jump, sure; he's almost ready now. Don and the other hounds will tree him again pretty soon. If he runs up the canyon, well and good. Then, if you can get the lasso on the other, I'll yell for Emett to come up to help you, and I'll follow Don."

Jones began the ascent of the piñon. The branches were not too close, affording him easy climbing. Before we looked for even a move on the part of the lions, the lower one began stepping down. I yelled a warning, but Jones did not have time to take advantage of it. He had half turned, meaning to swing out and drop, when the lion planted both fore paws upon his back. Jones went sprawling down, with the lion almost on him.

ROPING LIONS IN THE GRAND CANYON

● ● ●

Don had his teeth in the lion before he touched the ground, and when he did strike the rest of the hounds were on him. A cloud of dust rolled down the slope. The lion broke loose and with great, springy bounds ran up the canyon, Don and his followers hotfooting it after him.

Moze and Sounder broke the dead sapling to which I had tied them and, dragging it behind them, endeavored in frenzied action to join the chase. I drew them back, loosening the rope, so in case the other lion jumped I could free them quickly.

Jones calmly gathered himself up, rearranged his lasso, took his long stick, and proceeded to mount the piñon again. I waited till I saw him slip the noose over the lion's head, then I ran down the slope to yell for Emett. He answered at once. I told him to hurry to Jones's assistance. With that I headed up the canyon.

I hung close to the broad trail left by the lion and his pursuers. I passed perilously near the brink of precipices, but fear of them was not in me that day. I passed out of the Bay into the mouth of Left Canyon, and began to climb. The baying of the hounds directed me. In the box of yellow walls the chorus seemed to come from a hundred dogs.

When I found them, close to a low cliff, baying the lion in a thick, dark piñon, Ranger leaped into my arms, and next Don stood up against me with his

● ● ●

paws on my shoulders. These were strange actions, and, though I marked it at the moment, I had ceased to wonder at our hounds. I took one picture as the lion sat in the dark shade, and then climbed to the low cliff and sat down. I called Don to me and held him. In case our quarry leaped upon the cliff I wanted a hound to put quickly on his trail.

Another hour passed. It must have been a dark hour for the lion—he looked as if it were—and one of impatience for the baying hounds, but for me it was a full hour. Alone with the hounds and a lion, far from the walks of men, walled in by the wild-colored cliffs, with the dry, sweet smell of cedar and piñon, I asked no more.

Sounder and Moze, vociferously venting their arrival, were forerunners to Jones. I saw his gray locks waving in the breeze, and yelled for him to take his time. As he reached me the lion jumped and ran up the canyon. This suited me, for I knew he would take to a tree soon and the farther up he went the less distance we would have to pack him. From the cliff I saw him run up a slope, pass a big cedar, cunningly turn on his trail, and then climb into the tree and hide in its thickest part. Don passed him, got off the trail, and ran at fault. The others, so used to his leadership, were also baffled. But Jude, crippled and slow, brought up the rear, and she did not go a yard beyond where the lion turned. She opened up her deep call

● ● ●

under the cedar, and in a moment the howling pack were around her.

Jones and I toiled laboriously upward. He had brought my lasso, and he handed it to me with the significant remark that I would soon have need of it.

The cedar was bushy and overhung a yellow, bare slope that made Jones shake his head. He climbed the tree, lassoed the spitting lion and then leaped down to my side. By united and determined efforts we pulled the lion off the limb and let him down. The hounds began to leap at him. We both roared in a rage at them, but to no use.

"Hold him there!" shouted Jones, leaving me with the lasso while he sprang forward.

The weight of the animal dragged me forward and, had I not taken a half hitch round a dead snag, would have lifted me off my feet or pulled the lasso from my hands. As it was, the choking lion, now within reach of the furious, leaping hounds, swung to and fro before my face. He could not see me, but his frantic lunges narrowly missed me.

If never before, Jones then showed his genius. Don had hold of the lion's flank, and Jones, grabbing the hound by the hind legs, threw him down the slope. Don fell and rolled a hundred feet before he caught himself. Then Jones threw old Moze rolling, and Ranger, and all except faithful Jude. Before they could get back he roped the lion again and made fast

● ● ●

to a tree. Then he yelled for me to let go. The lion fell. Jones grabbed the lasso, at the same time calling for me to stop the hounds. As they came bounding up the steep slope, I had to club the noble fellows into submission.

Before the lion recovered wholly from his severe choking, we had his paws bound fast. Then he could only heave his tawny sides, glare and spit at us.

"Now what?" asked Jones. "Emett is watching the second lion, which we fastened by chain and lasso to a swinging branch. I'm all in. My heart won't stand any more climb."

"You go to camp for the pack horses," I said briefly. "Bring them all, and all the packs, and Navvy, too. I'll help Emett tie up the second lion, and then we'll pack them both up here to this one. You take the hounds with you."

"Can you tie up that lion?" asked Jones. "Mind you, he's loose except for a collar and chain. His claws haven't been clipped. Besides, it'll be an awful job to pack those two lions up here."

"We can try," I said. "You hustle to camp. Your horse is right up back of here, across the point, if I don't mistake my bearings."

Jones, admonishing me again, called the hounds and wearily climbed the slope. I waited until he was out of hearing, then began to retrace my trail down into the canyon. I made the descent in quick time, to

● ● ●

find Emett standing guard over the lion. The beast had been tied to an overhanging branch that swung violently with every move he made.

"When I got here," said Emett, "he was hanging over the side of that rock, almost choked to death. I drove him into this corner between the rocks and the tree, where he has been comparatively quiet. Now, what's up? Where is Jones? Did you get the third lion?"

I related what had occurred, and then said we were to tie this lion and pack him with the other one up the canyon, to meet Jones and the horses.

"All right," replied Emett, with a grim laugh. "We'd better get at it. Now I'm some worried about the lion we left below. He ought to be brought up, but we both can't go. This lion here will kill himself."

"What will the other one weigh?"

"All of one hundred and fifty pounds."

"You can't pack him alone."

"I'll try, and I reckon that's the best plan. Watch this fellow and keep him in the corner."

Emett left me then, and I began a third long vigil beside a lion. The rest was more than welcome. An hour and a half passed before I heard the sliding of stones below, which told me that Emett was coming. He appeared on the slope almost bent double, carrying the lion, head downward, before him. He could

● ● ●

climb only a few steps without lowering his burden and resting.

I ran down to meet him. We secured a stout pole, and slipping this between the lion's paws, below where they were tied, we managed to carry him fairly well, and after several rests, got him up alongside the other.

"Now to tie that rascal!" exclaimed Emett. "Jones said he was the meanest one he'd tackled, and I believe it. We'll cut a piece off of each lasso, and unravel them so as to get strings. I wish Jones hadn't tied the lasso to that swinging branch."

"I'll go and untie it." Acting on this suggestion, I climbed the tree and started out on the branch. The lion growled fiercely.

"I'm afraid you'd better stop," warned Emett. "That branch is bending and the lion can reach you."

But despite this I slipped out a couple of yards farther, and had almost gotten to the knotted lasso, when the branch swayed and bent alarmingly. The lion sprang from his corner and crouched under me, snarling and spitting, with every indication of leaping.

"Jump! Jump! Jump!" shouted Emett hoarsely.

I dared not, for I could not jump far enough to get out of the lion's reach. I raised my legs and began to slide myself back up the branch. The lion leaped, missing me, but scattering the dead twigs. Then the beast, beside himself with fury, half leaped, half

● ● ●

stood up, and reached for me. I looked down into his blazing eyes and open mouth and saw his white fangs.

Everything grew blurred before my eyes. I desperately fought for control over mind and muscle. I heard hoarse roars from Emett. Then I felt a hot burning pain in my wrist, which stung all my faculties into keen life again.

I saw the lion's beaked claws fastened in my leather wristband. At the same instant Emett dashed under the branch and grasped the lion's tail. One powerful lunge of his broad shoulders tore the lion loose and flung him down the slope to the full extent of his lasso. Quick as thought I jumped down, and just in time to prevent Emett from attacking the lion with the heavy pole we had used.

"I'll kill him! I'll kill him!" roared Emett.

"No, you won't," I replied quietly, for my pain had served to soothe my excitement as well as to make me more determined. "We'll tie up the darned tiger, if he cuts us all to pieces. You know how Jones will give us the laugh if we fail. Here, bind up my wrist."

Mention of Jones's probable ridicule and sight of my injury cooled Emett.

"It's a nasty scratch," he said, binding my handkerchief round it. "The leather saved your hand from being torn off. He's an ugly brute, but you're right, we'll tie him. Now, let's each take a lasso and worry

● ● ●

him till we get hold of a paw. Then we can stretch him out."

Jones did a fiendish thing when he tied that lion to the swinging branch. It was almost worse than having him entirely free. He had a circle almost twenty feet in diameter in which he could run and leap at will. It seemed he was in the air all the time. First at Emett, then at me he sprang, mouth agape, eyes wild, claws spread. We whipped him with our nooses, but not one would hold. He always tore it off before we could draw it tight. I secured a precarious hold on one hind paw and straightened my lasso.

"That's far enough," cried Emett. "Now hold him tight; don't lift him off the ground."

I had backed up the slope. Emett faced the lion, noose ready, waiting for a favorable chance to rope a front paw. The lion crouched low and tense, only his long tail lashing back and forth across my lasso. Emett threw the loop in front of the spread paws, now half sunk into the dust.

"Ease up; ease up," said he. "I'll tease him to jump into the noose."

I let my rope sag. Emett poked a stick into the lion's face. All at once I saw the slack in the lasso which was tied to the lion's chain. Before I could yell to warn my comrade the beast leaped. My rope burned as it tore through my hands. The lion sailed into the air, his paws widespread like wings, and one

● ● ●

of them struck Emett on the head and rolled him on the slope. I jerked back on my rope only to find it had slipped its hold.

"He slugged me one," remarked Emett, calmly rising and picking up his hat. "Did he break the skin?"

"No, but he tore your hatband off," I replied. "Let's keep at him."

For a few moments or an hour—no one will ever know how long—we ran round him, raising the dust, scattering the stones, breaking the branches, dodging his onslaughts. He leaped at us to the full length of his tether, sailing right into our faces, a fierce, uncowed, tigerish beast. If it had not been for the collar and swivel he would have choked himself a hundred times. Quick as a cat, supple, powerful, tireless, he kept on the go, whirling, bounding, leaping, rolling, till it seemed we would never catch him.

"If anything breaks, he'll get one of us," cried Emett. "I felt his breath that time."

"Lord! How I wish we had some of those fellows here who say lions are rank cowards!" I exclaimed.

In one of his sweeping side swings the lion struck the rock and hung there on its flat surface with his tail hanging over.

"Attract his attention," shouted Emett, "but don't get too close. Don't make him jump."

While I slowly maneuvered in front of the lion, Emett slipped behind the rock, lunged for the long

• • •

tail and got a good hold of it. Then with a whoop he ran around the rock, carrying the kicking, squalling lion clear of the ground.

"Now's your chance," he yelled. "Rope a hind foot! I can hold him."

In a second I had a noose fast on both hind paws, and then passed my rope to Emett. While he held the lion I again climbed the tree, untied the knot that had caused so much trouble, and very shortly we had our obstinate captive stretched out between two trees. After that we took a much-needed breathing spell.

"Not very scientific," growled Emett, by way of apologizing for our crude work, "but we had to get him some way."

"Emett, do you know I believe Jones put up a job on us?" I said.

"Well, maybe he did. We had the job all right. But we'll make short work of him now."

He certainly went at it in a way that alarmed me and would have electrified Jones. While I held the chain Emett muzzled the lion with a stick and a strand of lasso. His big blacksmith's hands held, twisted and tied with remorseless strength.

"Now for the hardest part of it," said he, "packing him up."

We toiled and drudged upward, resting every few yards, wet with sweat, boiling with heat, parching for water. We slipped and fell, got up to slip and fall

● ● ●

again. The dust choked us. We senselessly risked our lives on the brinks of precipices. We had no thought save to get the lion up. One hour of unremitting labor saw our task finished, so far. Then we wearily went down for the other.

"This one is the heaviest," Emett said gloomily.

We had to climb partly sidewise with the pole in the hollow of our elbows. The lion dragged head downward, catching in the brush and on the stones. Our rests became more frequent. Emett, who had the downward end of the pole, and therefore thrice the weight, whistled when he drew breath. Half the time I saw red mist before my eyes. How I hated the sliding stones!

"Wait," panted Emett once. "You're—younger—than me—wait!"

For that Mormon giant—used all his days to strenuous toil, peril and privation—to ask me to wait for him, was a compliment which I valued more than any I had ever received.

At last we dropped our burden in the shade of a cedar where the other lions lay, and we stretched ourselves. A long, sweet rest came abruptly to end with Emett's next words.

"The lions are choking! They're dying of thirst! We must have water!"

One glance at the poor, gasping, frothing beasts proved to me the nature of our extremity.

• • •

"Water in this desert! Where will we find it? Oh, why did I forget my canteen!"

After all our hopes, our efforts, our tragedies, and finally our wonderful good fortune, to lose these beautiful lions for lack of a little water was sickening, maddening.

"Think quick!" cried Emett. "I'm no good; I'm all in. But you must find water. It snowed yesterday. There's water somewhere."

Into my mind flashed a picture of the many little pockets beaten by rains into the shelves and promontories of the canyon rim. With the thought I was on the jump. I ran; I climbed; I seemed to have wings; I reached the rim, and hurried along it with eager gaze. I swung down on a cedar branch to a projecting point of rock. Small depressions were everywhere still damp, but the water had evaporated. But I would not give up. I jumped from rock to rock, and climbed over scaly ledges, and set tons of yellow shale into motion. And I found on a ragged promontory many little, round holes, some a foot deep, all full of clear water. Using my handkerchief as a sponge, I filled my cap.

Then began my journey down. I carried the cap with both hands and balanced myself like a tightrope performer. I zigzagged the slopes; slipped over stones; leaped fissures and traversed yellow slides. I safely descended places that in an ordinary moment

● ● ●

would have presented insurmountable obstacles, and burst down upon Emett with an Indian yell of triumph.

"Good!" ejaculated he. If I had not known it already, the way his face changed would have told me of his love for animals. He grasped a lion by the ears and held his head up. I saturated my handkerchief and squeezed the water into his mouth. He wheezed, coughed, choked, but to our joy he swallowed. He had to swallow. One after the other we served them so, seeing with unmistakable relief the sure signs of recovery. Their eyes cleared and brightened; the dry coughing that distressed us so ceased; the froth came no more. The savage fellow that had fought us to a standstill, and for which we had named him Spitfire, raised his head, the gold in his beautiful eyes darkened to fire, and he growled his return to life and defiance.

Emett and I sank back in unutterable relief.

"Waa-hoo!" Jones's yell came, breaking the warm quiet of the slope. Our comrade appeared riding down. The voice of the Indian, calling to Marc, mingled with the ringing of iron-shod hoofs on the stones.

Jones surveyed the small level spot in the shade of the cedars. He gazed from the lions to us, his stern face relaxed, and his dry laugh cracked.

"Doggone me, if you didn't do it!"

13

A strange procession soon emerged from Left Canyon, and stranger to us than the lion heads bobbing out of the alfagoes was the sight of Navvy riding in front of the lions. I kept well in the rear, for if any thing happened, which I calculated was more than likely, I wanted to see it. Before we had reached the outskirts of pines, I observed that the piece of lasso around Spitfire's nose had worked loose.

Just as I was about to make this known to Jones, the lion opened a corner of his mouth and fastened his teeth in the Navajo's overalls. He did not catch the flesh, for when Navvy turned around he wore only an expression of curiosity. But when he saw

● ● ●

Spitfire chewing him he uttered a shrill scream and fell sidewise off his horse.

Then two difficulties presented themselves to us—to catch the frightened horse and persuade the Indian he had not been bitten. We failed in the latter. Navvy gave us and the lions a wide berth, and walked to camp.

Jim was waiting for us, and said he had chased a lion south along the rim till the hounds got away from him.

Spitfire, having already been chained, was the first lion we endeavored to introduce to our family of captives. He raised such a fearful row that we had to remove him some distance from the others.

"We have two dog chains," said Jones, "but not a collar or a swivel in camp. We can't chain the lions without swivels. They'd choke themselves in two minutes."

Once more, for the hundredth time, Emett came to our rescue with his inventive and mechanical skill. He took the largest pair of hobbles we had, and with an axe, a knife and Jones's wire nippers, fashioned two collars and swivels that for strength and service-ableness improved somewhat on those we had bought.

Darkness was enveloping the forest when we finished supper. I fell into my bed and, despite the throbbing and burning of my wrist, soon lapsed into slumber. And I crawled out next morning late for breakfast, stiff, worn out, crippled, but happy. Six lions roaring a concert for me was quite conducive to contentment.

Emett interestingly engaged himself on a new pair of trousers, which he had contrived to produce from two of our empty meal-bags. The lower half of his overalls had gone to decorate the cedar spikes and brush, and these new bag-leg trousers, while somewhat remarkable for design, answered the purpose well enough. Jones's coat was somewhere along the canyon rim, his shoes were full of holes, his shirt in strips, and his trousers in rags. Jim looked like a scarecrow. My clothes, being of heavy waterproofed duck, had stood the hard usage in a manner to bring forth the unanimous admiration of my companions.

"Well, fellows," said Jones, "there's six lions, and that's more than we can pack out of here. Have you had enough hunting? I have."

"And I," rejoined Emett.

"Shore you can bet I have," drawled Jim.

"One more day, boys, and then I've done," said I. "Only one more day!"

Signs of relief on the faces of my good comrades showed how they took this evidence of my satisfied ambition.

I spent all the afternoon with the lions, photographing them, listening to them spit and growl, watching them fight their chains, and roll up like balls of fire. From different parts of the forest I tried to creep unsuspected upon them; but always, when I peeped out from behind a tree or log, every pair of ears would be erect, every pair of eyes gleaming and suspicious.

Spitfire afforded more amusement than all the others. He had indeed the temper of a king; he had been born for sovereignty, not slavery. To intimidate me he tried every manner of expression and utterance, and, failing, he always ended with a spring in the air to the length of his chain. This means was always effective. I simply could not stand still when he leaped; and in turn I tried every artifice I could think of to make him back away from me, to take refuge behind his tree. I ran at him with a club as if I were going to kill him. He waited, crouching. Finally, in dire extremity, I bethought me of a red flannel hood that Emett had given me, saying I might use it on cold nights. This was indeed a weird, flaming headgear, falling like a cloak down over the shoulders. I put it on, and, camera in hand, started to crawl on all fours toward Spitfire.

I needed no one to tell me that this proceeding was entirely beyond his comprehension. In his astonishment he forgot to spit and growl, and he backed behind the little pine, from which he regarded me with growing perplexity. Then, having revenged myself on him and getting a picture, I left him in peace.

14

I awoke before dawn, and lay watching the dark shadows change into gray, and gray into light. The Navajo chanted solemnly and low his morning song. I got up with the keen eagerness of the hunter who faces the last day of his hunt.

I warmed my frozen fingers at the fire. A hot breakfast smoked on the red coals. We ate while Navvy fed and saddled the horses.

"Shore they'll be somethin' doin' today," said Jim, fatalistically.

"We haven't crippled a horse yet," put in Emett hopefully. Don led the pack and us down the ridge, out of the pines into the sage. The sun, a red ball, glared out of the eastern mist, shedding a dull glow

145

● ● ●

on the ramparts of the far canyon walls. A herd of white-tailed deer scattered before the hounds. Blue grouse whirred from under our horses' feet.

"Spread out," ordered Jones, and though he meant the hounds, we all followed his suggestion, as the wisest course.

Ranger began to work up the sage ridge to the right. Jones, Emett and I followed, while Jim rode away to the left. Gradually the space widened, and as we neared the cedars, a sharply defined, deep canyon separated us.

We heard Don open up, then Sounder. Ranger left the trail he was trying to work out in the thick sage, and bounded in the direction of the rest of the pack. We reined in to listen.

First Don, then Sounder, then Jude, then one of the pups bayed eagerly, telling us they were hunting hard. Suddenly the bays blended in one savage sound.

"Hi! Hi! Hi!" cracked the cool, thin air. We saw Jim wave his hand from the far side of the canyon, spur his horse into action, and disappear into the cedars.

"Stick close together," yelled Jones, as we launched forward. We made the mistake of not going back to cross the canyon, for the hounds soon went up the opposite side. As we rode on and on, the sounds of the chase lessened, and finally ceased. To

● ● ●

our great chagrin we found it necessary to retrace our steps, and when we did get over the deep gully, so much time had elapsed that we despaired of coming up with Jim. Emett led, keeping close on Jim's trail, which showed plain in the dust, and we followed.

Up and down ravines, over ridges, through sage flats and cedar forests, to and fro, around and around, we trailed Jim and the hounds. From time to time one of us let out a long yell.

"I see a big lion track," called Jones once, and that stirred us on faster. Fully an hour passed before Jones halted us, saying we had best try a signal. I dismounted, while Emett rolled his great voice through the cedars.

A long silence ensued. From the depths of the forest Jim's answer struck faintly on my ear. With a word to my companions I leaped on my mustang and led the way. I rode as far as I could mark a straight line with my eye, then stopped to wait for another cry. In this way, slowly but surely we closed in on Jim.

We found him on the verge of the Bay, in the small glade where I had left my horse the day I followed Don alone down the canyon. Jim was engaged in binding up the leg of his horse. The baying of the hounds floated up over the rim.

"What's up?" queried Jones.

"Old Sultan. That's what," replied Jim. "We run

• • •

plumb into him. We've had him in five trees. It ain't been long since he was in that cedar there. When he jumped the yellow pup was in the way an' got killed. My horse just managed to jump clear of the big lion, an' as it was, nearly broke his leg."

Emett examined the leg and pronounced it badly strained, and advised Jim to lead the horse back to camp. Jones and I stood a moment over the remains of the yellow pup, and presently Emett joined us.

"He was the most playful one of the pack," said Emett, and then he placed the limp, bloody body in a crack, and laid several slabs of stone over it.

"Hurry after the other hounds," said Jim. "That lion will kill them one by one. An' look out for him!"

If we needed an incentive, the danger threatening the hounds furnished one; but I calculated the death of the pup was enough. Emett had a flare in his eye, Jones looked darker and more grim than ever, and I had sensations that boded ill to old Sultan.

"Fellows," I said, "I've been down this place, and I know where the old brute has gone; so come on."

I laid aside my coat, chaps and rifle, feeling that the business ahead was stern and difficult. Then I faced the canyon. Down slopes, among rocks, under piñons, around yellow walls, along slides, the two big men followed me with heavy steps. We reached the white streambed, and sliding, slipping, jumping, always down and down, we came at last within sound

● ● ●

of the hounds. We found them baying wildly under a piñon on the brink of the deep cove.

Then, at once, we all saw old Sultan close at hand. He was of immense size; his color was almost gray; his head huge, his paws heavy and round. He did not spit, nor snarl, nor growl; he did not look at the hounds, but kept his half-shut eyes upon us.

We had no time to make a move before he left his perch and hit the ground with a thud. He walked by the baying hounds, looked over the brink of the cove, and, without an instant of hesitation, leaped down. The rattling crash of sliding stones came up with a cloud of dust. Then we saw him leisurely picking his way among the rough stones.

Exclamations from the three of us attested to what we thought of that leap.

"Look the place over," called Jones. "I think we've got him."

The cove was a hole hollowed out by running water. At its head, where the perpendicular wall curved, the height was not less than forty feet. The walls became higher as the cove deepened toward the canyon. It had a length of perhaps a hundred yards, and a width of perhaps half as many. The floor was mass on mass of splintered rock.

"Let the hounds down on a lasso," said Jones.

Easier said than done! Sounder, Ranger, Jude refused. Old Moze grumbled and broke away. But Don,

● ● ●

stern and savage, allowed Jones to tie him in a slip noose.

"It's a shame to send that grand hound to his death," protested Emett.

"We'll all go down," declared Jones.

"We can't. One will have to stay up here to help the other two out," replied Emett.

"You're the strongest; you stay up," said Jones. "Better work along the wall and see if you can locate the lion."

We let Don down into the hole. He kicked himself loose before reaching the bottom and then, yelping, he went out of sight among the boulders. Moze, as if ashamed, came whining to us. We slipped a noose around him and lowered him, kicking and barking, to the rocky floor. Jones made the lasso fast to a cedar root, and I slid down, like a flash, burning my hands. Jones swung himself over, wrapped his leg around the rope, and came down, to hit the ground with a thump. Then, lassos in hands, we began clambering over the broken fragments.

For a few moments we were lost to sights and sounds away from our immediate vicinity. The bottom of the cove afforded hard going. Dead piñons and cedars blocked our way; the great, jagged stones offered no passage. We crawled, climbed, and jumped from piece to piece.

A yell from Emett halted us. We saw him above,

● ● ●

on the extreme point of wall. Waving his arms, he yelled unintelligible commands to us. The fierce baying of Don and Moze added to our desperate energy.

The last jumble of splintered rock cleared, we faced a terrible and wonderful scene.

"Look! Look!" I gasped to Jones.

A wide, bare strip of stone lay a few yards beneath us; and in the center of this last step sat the great lion on his haunches with his long tail lashing out over the precipice. Back to the canyon, he confronted the furious hounds; his demeanor had changed to one of savage apprehension.

When Jones and I appeared, old Sultan abruptly turned his back to the hounds and looked down into the canyon. He walked the whole length of the bare rock with his head stretched over. He was looking for a niche or a step whereby he might again elude his foes.

Faster lashed his tail; farther and farther stretched his neck. He stopped, and with head bent so far over the abyss that it seemed he must fall, he looked and looked.

How grandly he fitted the savage sublimity of that place! The tremendous purple canyon depths lay beneath him. He stood on the last step of his mighty throne. The great downward slopes had failed him. Majestically and slowly he turned from the deep that offered no hope.

ROPING LIONS IN THE GRAND CANYON

● ● ●

As he turned, Jones cast the noose of his lasso perfectly round the burly neck. Sultan roared and worked his jaws, but he did not leap. Jones must have expected such a move, for he fastened his rope to a spur of rock. Standing there, revolver gripped, hearing the baying hounds, the roaring lion, and Jones's yells mingled with Emett's, I had no idea what to do. I was in a trance of sensations.

Old Sultan ran rather than leaped at us. Jones evaded the rush by falling behind a stone, but still did not get out of danger. Don flew at the lion's neck and Moze buried his teeth in a flank. Then the three rolled on the rock dangerously near the verge.

Bellowing, Jones grasped the lasso and pulled. Still holding my revolver, I leaped to his assistance, and together we pulled and jerked. Don got away from the lion with remarkable quickness. But Moze, slow and dogged, could not elude the outstretched paws, which fastened in his side and leg. We pulled so hard we slowly raised the lion. Moze, never whimpering, clawed and scratched at the rock in his efforts to escape. The lion's red tongue protruded from his dripping jaws. We heard the rend of hide as our efforts, combined with those of Moze, loosed him from the great yellow claws.

The lion, whirling and wrestling, rolled over the precipice. When the rope straightened with a twang, had it not been fastened to the rock, Jones and I

● ● ●

would have been jerked over the wall. The shock threw us to our knees.

For a moment we did not realize the situation. Emett's yells awakened us.

"Pull! Pull! Pull!" roared he.

Then, knowing that old Sultan would hang himself in a few moments, we attempted to lift him. Jones pulled till his back cracked; I pulled till I saw red before my eyes. Again and again we tried. We could lift him only a few feet. Soon exhausted, we had to desist altogether. How Emett roared and raged from his vantage point above! He could see the lion in death throes.

Suddenly he quieted down with the words: "All over; all over!" Then he sat still, looking into space. Jones sat mopping his brow. And I, all my hot resentment vanished, lay on the rock, with eyes on the distant mesas.

Presently Jones leaned over the verge with my lasso.

"There," he said, "I've roped one of his hind legs. Now we'll pull him up a little, then we'll fasten this rope, and pull on the other."

So, foot by foot, we worked the heavy lion up over the wall. He must have been dead, though his sides heaved. Don sniffed at him in disdain. Moze, dusty and bloody, with a large strip of hide hanging from his flank, came up growling low and deep, and gave the lion a last vengeful bite.

"We've been fools," observed Jones, meditatively. "The excitement of the game made us lose our wits. I'll never rope another lion."

I said nothing. While Moze licked his bloody leg and Don lay with his fine head on my knees, Jones began to skin old Sultan. Once more the strange, infinite silence enfolded the canyon. The far-off golden walls glistened in the sun; farther down, the purple clefts smoked. The many-hued peaks and mesas, aloof from each other, rose out of the depths. It was a grand and gloomy scene of ruin where every glistening descent of rock was but a page of earth's history.

It brought to my mind a faint appreciation of what time really meant; it spoke of an age of former men; it showed me the lonesome crags of eagles, and the cliff lairs of lions; and it taught mutely, eloquently, a lesson of life—that men are still savage, still driven by a spirit to roam, to hunt, and to slay.